Sue Flavell has lived in Englanc
USA.

A journalist and scriptwriter, she has also worked in the theatre, book and magazine publishing and on documentary films.

Her memoir of a country childhood – "Where the Brook and River Meet" – was published in 1994 and serialised on radio.

To Sally
with love

Sue
x

DOING THE CONTINENTAL

Sue Flavell

_____

Doing the Continental

Copyright © 2008 Sue Flavell

For my mother and father.

ACKNOWLEDGEMENTS

My thanks to Janis Mitchell for the cover illustrations, Simon Nicholson for graphic design, and Hilary Hammond, Sue Cottingham, Joy Yaffe and Olga Yaffe for their enthusiastic support.

CHAPTER ONE

Ronald Lucas had gone to meet his Maker on an empty stomach. It was his wife's fault. Dinner hadn't been ready on time. Something had distracted Dotty, as usual. Patient as always, he'd squeezed her arm, said it didn't matter - that he'd have another twenty minutes pottering in the garden.

When, finally, the roast lamb and home-grown potatoes, beans and carrots were on the table, Dotty had called him from the kitchen door. But there'd been no reply. Ronald's pottering was total absorption. He could lose himself in his gardening just as completely as Dotty could lose herself in - well, in whatever had seduced her away from the chore in hand.

She'd crossed the lawn, savouring the unseasonal softness of the early evening air, and found Ronald lying in the vegetable garden. Dotty had known he was dead even before she felt for his pulse. If he had to die now, then this was the way he would have chosen, she thought: earth on his face, his glasses pushed up onto his forehead; the lenses still intact. Ronald always did everything carefully and even when breathing his last had somehow contrived to fall softly.

As if on autopilot, Dotty had walked down the

path to the garden shed and brought out a faded tartan travelling rug which had lived there for almost as long as she and Ronald had lived in the house; its scent sweetly redolent of years of children's picnics on the lawn, of newly mown grass.

Turning his head slightly, she'd gently removed his glasses and closed his eyes. Unable to bear the finality of putting the rug over his head, she'd tucked it tenderly around his body - as if she'd come upon him unexpectedly taking a nap and covered him for warmth.

Returning to the house, she'd calmly telephoned the doctor and her daughters, Angela and Jenny, then sat waiting for them at the kitchen table, the smell of roast lamb in her nostrils, the buttered vegetables cooling in their dishes, the table laid for two.

******

That had been four days ago. Now, lying in bed, sipping hot milk with a dash of whisky, listening to the clock on the tower of St. Botolph's striking midnight, Dotty still couldn't mourn. Mourn as she'd always believed every woman would mourn the death of a dearly loved husband: floods of tears, hysteria perhaps, surrounded by pale, concerned faces. Just because Ronald had bored her for much of their forty-odd years of marriage, smiled indulgently whenever she suggested they do something exciting for a change but then disappeared, as usual, into his greenhouse each weekend, she hadn't stopped loving him.

During the numerous ritual tasks - registering the death, informing the undertaker, discussing with the vicar the choice of hymns for the funeral - she'd been suspended, despite the presence of her daughters, in a thick cloud of culinary regret, her head filled with a ceaseless refrain:

"Ronald died on an empty stomach...he missed his last supper...no more bread and butter pudding."

She'd found it in the oven the following morning, sunk and sad, and spent twenty minutes mindlessly scraping the Pyrex dish clean until, satisfied, she could hold it up to the light and see it sparkle. Just like in those stupid television commercials for washing-up liquids.

Dotty hadn't felt guilty on that fateful evening about being late with dinner, knowing she'd made a bread and butter pudding - Ronald's favourite. Truth was, she mused now with one of those insights which so often torment one at such a time, she'd never felt guilty until the moment Ronald died; the moment when it was too late.

Perhaps, she wondered, this obsessive concern

with Ronald's stomach was the result of being a housewife for all those years; her life revolving around the planning and preparation of food, whether it was on time or not. It had never mattered to Ronald and it wouldn't have mattered this time. No doubt, arriving in Heaven, for as sure as hell Ronald would have gone to Heaven, he'd have been well looked after.

"Hello Ronald," says God. "Welcome to Heaven. Had a decent trip up?"

"Very smooth, thank you," says Ronald, courteous to the end.

"I'm sure you'll soon settle in," says God, "but if you need anything, just give me a shout."

"Well," says Ronald, not wanting to make a fuss so soon after his arrival, but knowing you shouldn't lie to God, "If truth be told, I'm absolutely famished."

No, thought Dotty, Ronald wouldn't have needed to tell God he was hungry. God is All Knowing. If Ronald's number was up, like the ones she took at the cheese counter in the supermarket to await her turn, God would have been expecting him to arrive hungry, would have known he had a scatterbrained wife, who, at long last, would be feeling guilty. "Thanks very much, God!" she muttered, as she turned to put her empty mug on the bedside table.

And, as sure as eggs were eggs, she thought , with

a pang of regret on Ronald's behalf, Heaven would be a meat-free zone. All God's Creatures. No more roast lamb up there. The place would be seething with animal rights loonies. Still, Ronald would be able to tell them about his prize-winning vegetables.

Dotty smiled and caught herself smiling. It was no laughing matter. Strange how the darkest moments in life were so often reduced to absurdities. Perhaps it was Nature's way. Perhaps everyone at a time of personal grief chastised themselves for sins of omission; indulged in childish flights of fancy. Anyway, if the meal *had* been ready on time, Ronald might have fallen face down into his bread and butter pudding rather than taken a nose dive into his richly cultivated earth.

With that consoling thought Dotty turned off the bedside light and fell asleep with surprising rapidity, her mind at rest. In the middle of the night she awoke, startled, wondering in a split second of panic where she was. Then she made out the faint but familiar outline of the old, scratched tallboy, and turned instinctively to snuggle herself back to sleep wrapped around Ronald. But Ronald wasn't there. It was at this moment Dotty knew he would never be there again. No more cuddles. No more falling asleep in exasperation as Ronald, still propped up on his pillows, pen torch strapped to his forehead so he wouldn't disturb her, studied his seed catalogues with rapt delight. The tears began to fall and didn't stop until she was too exhausted to cry any more.

When her daughters visited in the morning and saw her swollen, stricken face, their sympathy was intensified by a feeling of relief.

Dotty watched Angela and Jenny walking down the drive to the street, grateful for their loving concern but pleased that she had persuaded them to get on with their own day and leave her alone with her thoughts. They had both offered to sleep at the house following their father's death but she'd insisted that she preferred to be alone, secretly disconcerted by her seeming inability to openly express her grief. Now she was relieved that when the tears *had* fallen she'd been able to give in to them without stifling her howls for fear of waking the family and intensifying their own sense of loss.

They were good daughters, she thought with gratitude, and seemed to be content; Angela married to Paul and the mother of her much-loved grandson, Richard. Paul was a bit pompous for her liking but he was a caring husband and father. Jenny seemed to be coming to terms with her divorce now and had mentioned a new boyfriend, an estate agent called Nick, whom Dotty hadn't as yet met. She hoped, with some feeling, that he'd be nicer than the last one.

It was one of life's sad ironies that the men to whom Jenny was attracted were equally self-centred and unlikely to give her the attention she craved. Angela had inherited her father's placid nature and in an age when women were trying to juggle family and career, had chosen to combine voluntary activities in the community with looking after her home.

Returning to the sitting room, Dotty stared at Ronald. He was wearing an endearingly proud grin and balancing a giant onion on each hand. The photograph, on the shabby Victorian mantelpiece, was flanked by rows of silver and gold cups proof, as if proof were needed, that Ronald not only won prizes for his fruit and vegetables but won again and again and again.

The trophies were already dulled by a few days' neglect. Wondering idly how many hours of her life had been spent polishing them, she gradually became aware of a faint but persistent trilling. She didn't like these modern, light-weight telephones with their grovelling little squeals. She preferred the old fashioned black bakelite telephones with their strident, intrusive brassiness, giving the impression that someone interesting with important news to impart might be on the other end. These days it was usually a double-glazing salesman or Oscar's Photographic Studio in the shopping precinct offering a ten per cent discount on family portraits so heavily touched up everyone looked like the waxworks at Madame Tussauds.

It was Margaret, always in mid-prattle before whoever she was calling had time to put the receiver to their ear. She lived in a permanent state of exasperation at Dotty's inability to organise her life. "Oh, I wouldn't do that dear," was her favourite refrain; the best possible reason, in Dotty's opinion, why she should do it. Perhaps that was why their friendship had endured. Dotty going her own chaotic way and often exaggerating her cock-ups just for the joy of seeing Margaret's censorious expression; and Margaret, perversely fascinated by Dotty's lack of inhibition, always anticipating the day when, she was convinced, Dotty would finally come a real cropper.

"Thank you, Margaret," said Dotty wearily when she could finally get a word in edgeways. "I'm coping very well, and I am *not* going to change my mind about burying Ronald. Cremation may be more hygienic, as you say, but I can't cremate Ronald, he's got a pacemaker. Incinerator doors blow off when pacemakers explode in the fiery furnace."

Dotty held the receiver away from her ear as she

heard the anguished squeal of horror. Serves her right, she thought grimly. Only Margaret would ring up on the day before the funeral and suggest that there was a nicer way of organising Ronald's send-off. Even the dead couldn't escape the benefit of her advice.

"I'm not being tasteless. Don't you read the papers? Eleven bricks ripped out of a crematorium wall last week. Killed one of the mourners. I want Ronald safely six feet under, not taking off like a Scud missile...And no," she added in answer to Margaret's enquiry - didn't she ever give up? - "I'm *not* going to remove the pacemaker. Ronald might need it where he's going...I mean gone," she finished lamely in some confusion.

Dotty said she'd see Margaret at St. Botolph's in the morning and hung up wondering why she was always supposed to be the disorganised one. She'd read about the problem with pacemakers. She was doing what she thought was right in the circumstances. Why didn't someone occasionally give her credit?

The doorbell rang. She went into the hall to answer it. A large, looming presence was visible through the stained-glass window of the door leading to the outside porch. Opening the door Dotty found Geoffrey standing on the doorstep. It was hard to believe that the scruffy, scabby-kneed little boy from next door whom Ronald had all too frequently admonished for scrumping his prize Comice pears was now six-foot three of solemnly self-important Police Constable Whitlow.

As Dotty opened the door wider to allow Geoffrey to step inside, he took two steps forward, carefully removing his helmet as he did so.

"I just wanted to say how very sorry I was to hear about…er…Mr. Lucas," he said in appropriately funereal tones, although Dotty knew that his sadness was genuine. "Bit sudden, like."

"It was. Keeled over in the vegetable garden."

"Well, I suppose it was the way he would have wanted to go," said Geoffrey, with a perception that surprised her.

"Yes," replied Dotty. "Flat out by the compost heap."

Geoffrey winced. "The Gardening Club's going to miss its champion."

"I wouldn't be so sure about that. Ronald won the cup seven years running. Maybe someone else thinks he'll be in with a chance now."

For a young man who had always found it difficult to articulate his feelings, Dotty's blunt honesty never ceased to shock him. He turned to leave and then, remembering something, turned back and handed Dotty a set of car keys. "I've put your car in the garage," he said.

"Oh you are a good boy," said Dotty.

Geoffrey gulped before saying what he'd planned to say, although trying to be authoritative with Dotty was far from easy. "I know this isn't the best time to say this Mrs. Lucas, but you've got to stop parking on that patch of grass by the entrance to the Police Car Pound. My Sergeant complained again today, said it couldn't go on."

"But it's so convenient, Geoffrey," replied Dotty, not pleased at being thwarted. "It's impossible to find a space in the High Street and if I park illegally you'll tow me to the Pound anyway, so I'm saving you the trouble really. Your Sergeant should be grateful."

Somewhat cowed by this logic, nevertheless Geoffrey persisted. "It wouldn't be so bad if you'd remember to collect your car more often."

"Sometimes I forget," said Dotty airily. "Other times if I've finished up at the far end of the High Street for coffee with Mrs. Matthews it's quicker to get a lift home with her."

"And you shouldn't leave the keys inside," said Geoffrey.

"If I can't trust the police with them, who can I trust," said Dotty indignantly. "Anyway," she went on, ignoring Geoffrey's startled eyes, "I thought you'd always found it quite handy, living next door, to drive home in my car instead of having to take the bus."

"But I've had a motor bike for a week, Mrs. Lucas," said Geoffrey, a whining note of youthful complaint entering his voice, "I've now got to go back on the bus to fetch my bike."

CHAPTER TWO

Dotty gazed out of the car window as she returned home after the funeral with her son-in-law, grandson and elder daughter, Angela. She was surprised to see that Belmont Avenue where she'd lived her entire married life still looked the same. She had somehow expected it to have taken on a different aspect now that Ronald, or rather his body, had been committed to the ground and the life she had known gone for ever. Since leaving the cemetery the family had been silent, no doubt occupied with their own thoughts about what had just taken place.

"Do you think that the vicar would give me permission to plant a fruit tree beside Ronald's grave?" asked Dotty, breaking the silence.

Paul, having known his mother-in-law for twenty years, was usually wary of any seemingly innocent suggestions she made. But he felt a rush of warmth towards her. It was a touchingly appropriate thought for a man who had been such a champion gardener.

"I think it would be a fitting memorial for him to rest in its shade," he replied, although secretly harbouring doubts that the authorities would allow it.

"Oh I wasn't thinking about *shade*," said Dotty

scathingly, "Shade's not going to be much use to Ronald now. I just thought it would be lovely for him to come back as an apple."

The car swerved. Paul quickly managed to correct it. Will I never learn, he thought, grimly.

Richard smiled, and Dotty thought for the millionth time how much she adored her only grandchild. He was seventeen now, like a young sapling himself. Throughout his life, Dotty had been his dearest confident; nothing shocked or surprised her and, too often in Paul's opinion, she'd taken Richard's side when his father had tried to impose discipline. Fellow conspirators, Paul had said of them to Angela more times than he cared to remember.

"If you had the same grasp of biochemistry as Gran has," Richard said to his father, "you'd realise that..."

"...that Ronald's goodness would seep into the roots of the tree," interrupted Dotty, "and..."

Paul braked fiercely, bringing the car to an abrupt halt in front of the house. It served, to his intense relief, to silence his mother-in-law..

It caused the driver of the Porsche following behind, in which Dotty's younger daughter Jenny was a passenger, to mutter a loud oath as he slammed on his brakes to avoid a collision.

"Damned fool," said Nick, staring through the

windscreen as Paul emerged from his car looking distressed.

"Paul's usually such a careful driver," said Jenny.

Nick turned off the engine with one hand and picked up his mobile with the other.

"Surely your call can wait!" Jenny said sharply.

"You go in. I'll only be a moment."

"It's nothing more than an umbilical cord."

"Don't be so intense. I just want to call the office; to touch base."

"Can't you think of anything other than selling houses?" Jenny replied. She wrenched open the car door and stormed up the path to the house, following in the wake of the rest of her family. Nick watched her as he waited for his secretary to come on the line.

"Nickers here," he said when Ginny answered. "Any news about the Miller's Lane property?"

"Talbot's agreed to pay the asking price," said Ginny.

"Excellent. I'm outside The Grove. I think we'll be instructed to handle the sale. Jenny's mother owns it. It's much too big for a widow. We could slot her into Safehaven as soon as there's a vacancy."

"She could buy number 25," said Ginny.

"No she can't. Old Blacklock's in there."

"Not any more he isn't."

"That retirement village is turning into a

goldmine. No sooner do we sell a flat to a Wrinklie than it's back on the market." Leaning forward, Nick opened the glove compartment and pulled out a newspaper folded over at the obituary column. "I'm looking in on that funeral at St. Clements this afternoon," he said, glancing at the newspaper." See if I can find out who's going to inherit 54 Meredith Road."

The Reverend Henderson, who, according to Margaret, "did a lovely funeral," was standing by the french windows gazing out over the Lucas's garden. He turned to Dotty as she brought him his favourite tipple, a double scotch, and thanked her profusely.

"Whenever I think of your dear, departed husband, I am reminded of Adam in the Garden of Eden," he said.

"If it'd been Ronald in the Garden of Eden the human race would have been extinct before it even got started," said Dotty. "He'd never have noticed Eve unless she'd offered to bottle his produce."

"The church's bring and buy sales would have been diminished without your jams and chutneys," replied the vicar in soothing tones. "Marriage to Mr. Lucas must have given you a very full and happy life."

"I didn't always want what it was full of, Vicar,"

said Dotty, jumping as she felt a dig in her ribs and turned to find Margaret beside her.

"I'm sure you won't mind my saying this, dear," said Margaret, "but I don't think *The Day Thou gavest, Lord, has ended* was an appropriate hymn to choose for a service at 11.30 in the morning."

"It was Ronald's favourite," said Dotty, "and he had a perfect right to have it sung on this of all days. We couldn't very well have buried him in the dark."

Angela and Paul, standing by the fireplace, watched Dotty move away with a grim expression on her face.

"Your father was such a stable character," said Paul quietly, "I've never understood how he coped with your mother all these years.

"She might have exasperated him sometimes but she never bored him," said Angela, giving Paul a look which he found disconcerting.

"Even so, she doesn't have to be quite so oblivious to convention. Tossing a single red rose into the grave after the coffin was lowered would have been rather a charming gesture, but lobbing in a couple of your father's prize onions and yelling 'Bet God's aren't as big as yours, Ronald' was highly embarrassing."

Richard, who had come over to join his parents, sniggered.

"It's not funny, Richard," said Paul.

"Lighten up, Dad, Gran's great."

Angela, seeing Margaret move towards Jenny and knowing how prickly her younger sister could be, thought it might be diplomatic to join them. As she did so, Margaret was giving her seal of approval to Nick.

"Such an attractive man," she was saying. "The Reverend Henderson does a lovely wedding."

"And Smithers, West and Drew did me a very nice divorce," said Jenny, with a bitterness which saddened Angela.

"Perhaps next time you could go through the first part without going through the second, dear," said Margaret brightly. "He must have a very nice home, being an estate agent."

"Nick lives in little better than a broom cupboard. He can't resist a good offer. He once invited me to dinner and when I arrived there was a note pinned to the door with a forwarding address..." Jenny tailed off, her eyes suddenly widening as she spotted Nick in the hall. He had a notebook and pen in his hands and was pacing out the black and white tiles, taking rough measurements.

"You have a knack of picking the least appropriate moments to do things," said Jenny furiously, as she strode into the hall and grabbed Nick by the arm.

"This is a wondrous house, darling," said Nick, shaking her off.

"And the first time you visit it my father has just died and you're planning to evict my mother," replied Jenny, grabbing his arm again and pulling him out of sight of the assembled mourners in the sitting room.

"Pure, untouched Victoriana," said Nick, ignoring her remark, "with an amazing conservatory. These large, shabby houses are at a premium."

"Will you get it through your thick skull that my mother is not going to sell it," Jenny replied, just as Dotty appeared from the kitchen holding a newly opened bottle of wine.

"What's that about selling?" she asked.

Jenny glared at Nick, willing him to remain silent.

"I'm very sorry about the loss of your husband, Mrs. Lucas," Nick said, not taking Jenny's hint, "but if it's any consolation to you, you've got a very valuable property here."

"Nick, for heaven's sake, not now," hissed Jenny, infuriated by his lack of sensitivity.

But Dotty was looking interested and Nick was not going to lose a potential client. "You could buy an apartment at Safehaven, the new retirement village. Tea dances on Wednesday afternoons, mini-golf course…beautifully appointed."

"How much?"

"About three hundred and fifty thousand."

"Good Heavens. I couldn't possibly afford that."

"No, Mrs. Lucas, you've misunderstood. I meant for *your* house."

Dotty stared at Nick. "You can't be serious," she said faintly.

"Ideal family house. Close to the shops. Large garden. Safe neighbourhood. We might even get more. I can think of a number of possible purchasers on our mailing list."

"But," said Jenny, annunciating her words carefully, "Mum is not going to sell."

———————

CHAPTER THREE

Later that year, Dotty woke early one morning in a state of high anticipatory excitement. At last she was free to act upon the momentous decision she had made when Nick told her, after the funeral, what the house was worth.

She realised in a brief and uncharacteristic moment of self-pity that she hadn't felt this excited since she was a child, waking on Christmas morning, seeing the shadowy bulge of a stocking hanging from the bedpost. The difference this time, she acknowledged ruefully, was that she'd be giving herself a present. But then, in truth, she hadn't often received what she'd hoped for as a child, her parents' income being modest.

Things hadn't improved much after her marriage. Ronald's first Christmas gift to her had been a pair of slippers. Disappointed but not wishing to hurt his feelings and hiding her own, she'd praised the originality of his gift. Every subsequent Christmas she'd received another pair.

As their wedding anniversary coincided with the eve of the annual gardening show, Ronald had always been too preoccupied to remember it. One year, when he was tucked up on a little truckle bed in the greenhouse, guarding his prize specimens overnight, Dotty had taken him a mug of hot chocolate. Wearing a shapeless old dressing gown, her hair in rollers, she'd stuck a homemade paper hat on top of them on which she'd scrawled *Happy Anniversary to Me.* Ronald had smiled fondly at her little joke, thanked her for the drink, and asked her to admire his marrow.

"It's a wonder, Ronald," Dotty murmured now, gazing at his photograph on the bedside table, "that I never hit you over the head with one."

But today, thought Dotty, as she pulled back the bedclothes, she was going to have exactly what she wanted. The house was sold - thanks to Nick. She'd sworn him to secrecy, knowing that if the family were aware of her real plans they'd have interfered.

Later that morning she drove down the High Street in her battered Mini, hurtled into a space beside a prominent NO PARKING sign, and picked up a piece of white card she'd placed beside her on the passenger seat. Just as she was propping it up on the dashboard she noticed Geoffrey Whitlow leaning over the bonnet, staring at the one word scrawled across it. Just my luck, she thought, as he walked round the side of the car and addressed her through the open sun roof.

"Since when have you been a journalist, Mrs. Lucas?"

"Since you stopped me parking at the Police Car Pound," replied Dotty with some asperity. "The

Press can park anywhere. Even on the pavement when they're covering a murder."

"No they can't," said Geoffrey. "You'll have to move this car."

"Yes Geoffrey."

"And don't let me see you using a fake Press Card again."

"Yes, I mean no, Geoffrey."

"And," he added kindly, "if you're quick, a car's just pulling out of a *legal* parking space a bit further down the road on the right."

Dotty glanced up at his face still looming over her. "You're a good lad," she said and blew him a kiss.

"That's as maybe," he replied, stepping back as she put the car into gear. "But it wouldn't hurt when you see me in uniform to address me as Constable."

Dotty was still smiling at Geoffrey's remark as she slipped into the parking space. Unlike an increasing number of local lads who preferred to hang around the pubs rather than do an honest day's work, he deserved her respect. She really must try to remember to do as he'd asked.

Determined not to inadvertently betray the reason why she was here today, Dotty decided that rather than walk down the High Street and risk bumping into friends, she'd take the back alley beside the supermarket. That way she could emerge directly opposite the place she had fantasised about for so many years and which she was shortly going to enter for the first time.

And there it was, facing her across the street as she emerged from the alley. A small, old-fashioned shop front, unchanged since the shopping parade was built in the 30's; it's sign board dwarfed by those of a chemist on one side and a building society on the other: NIGEL FAIRBROTHER. PAINLESS TRAVEL.

Taking a deep breath, Dotty crossed the road and went inside. A diminutive young man, bespectacled, wearing a neat suit, spotless white shirt and green bow tie was seated in front of a computer, concentrating fiercely. Rather than displaying the usual exaggeratedly colourful travel posters, the antiseptic cream walls were unadorned except for a prominent notice warning customers of the dangers of travelling without insurance. The room hummed with gleaming modern equipment: computers, printers, fax machine, television, DVD. On the young man's desk was a box of tissues, a regimented row of pill bottles and a carafe of water.

Dotty felt childishly let down. For so many years she'd thought of this little shop as the gateway to a whole world of exotic sights and new experiences and here she was in what looked like an intensive care unit. She seated herself on a chair facing the young man's desk irritated that, as yet, there had been no acknowledgement of her presence. Service with a smile was a thing of the past, she thought sadly. She cleared her throat. There was no response.

"Good morning," said Dotty brightly, "I want to go abroad."

"I wouldn't if I were you," said Nigel Fairbrother not looking up from his computer screen. "It's a very dangerous place is abroad."

"I am determined to see Europe before I die," said Dotty with dramatic emphasis, infuriated by his lack of interest.

"It will probably hasten your end, Madam," said Nigel, still staring at his computer screen.

He's been set up, thought Dotty in exasperation. There could be no other explanation. The family must have got to him first, suspecting she might try to break out. They'd obviously checked the *Yellow Pages* for travel agents within easy distance and then, dividing up the list between them, set off early to visit them all. 'If Mrs. Dorothy Lucas, Dotty by name and dotty by nature, should enter your esteemed premises...' she imagined Paul saying... The thought made her angry. It was her life. She refused to be beaten.

"You seem to have forgotten," said Dotty," about

the romance of travel."

Nigel suddenly looked up, startled, his eyes heavily magnified by his spectacles.

"Romance?" he squeaked "Romance? People pick up a brochure and next thing you know they've booked a ticket to somewhere they've never been and which may not even exist. They're packed on to aeroplanes, from which engines frequently fall off, or on to trains, which have a nasty habit of being derailed, or on to buses, which travel on the wrong side of the road, to reach some half-finished concrete jungle. Within twenty-four hours they've succumbed to sunstroke, been stung by jellyfish, eaten by sharks, mown down by speedboats, fallen off cliffs, or been trapped in a political coup. That's if they haven't already been flattened by Acts of God. If they're not carried home on stretchers suffering from horrible foreign diseases, they're exhausted by delays or been made bankrupt. Now what right-minded person wants to go through all *that?"*

"I do!" yelled Dotty, making Nigel jump.

They were reduced to a stunned silence by the exchange. Nigel reached across his desk and gulped down a tumbler of water, seemingly overcome by his volubility. Dotty, now in a state of considerable confusion, could feel her heart thumping. Surely the family couldn't have persuaded Nigel to go to these extremes? But if not, what was going on? Her experience of travel agents was sadly non-existent, but surely they weren't in the business of discouraging people from travelling?

Nigel, sensing her thoughts, apologised. "I always make that set speech to new customers," he said, "so they're forewarned."

"The thing is," said Dotty plaintively, "I've never, ever been anywhere for a holiday other than Bournemouth. My husband wouldn't go abroad."

"Nor will I," replied Nigel cheerfully, "not since I was eight and had my nasty trauma. Mum took me on a cross-channel ferry and we ran into a storm so bad we couldn't get into port for twenty-four hours."

Nigel held out a tube of peppermints and Dotty took one; her maternal feelings aroused by Nigel's solemn little face.

"You're not what I expected a travel agent to be like," she said gently.

"Mum wanted me to be a surgeon," said Nigel, "but blood makes me faint. Nigel, I asked myself, what's the next best thing? Well, it was obvious."

"What was?" asked Dotty, mystified.

"A travel agent also has the public's life in his hands. One mistake and cheerio." Nigel waved his arm, proudly indicating his computers. "I've got a state of the art intelligence network here, you know. Outbreaks of foreign diseases and weather reports are updated hourly. Even the age of aircraft. I won't let any client of mine fly on a plane that's more than five years old, which somewhat reduces your choice of destination, I suppose. Still, I've never lost a client yet. Not," he added mournfully, "that I get very many."

As Dotty listened to Nigel, her former bewilderment was replaced by a sense of elation. He was, she realised, her gift from the gods. Although she'd always felt her family exaggerated her impulsiveness, nevertheless, if she was about to embark upon the biggest adventure of her life she was honest enough to recognise that she was going to need all the help she could get. She knew with serene conviction that Nigel would organise her trip conscientiously; that she could rely upon him to watch over her.

"Nigel," she said, "I think you're wonderful."

"Pardon?" said Nigel, blushing furiously.

"You and I were meant for each other. Let's plan my trip."

"First things first, Madam," he replied nervously, putting up his tiny hands as if to ward off Dotty. "Don't let's get carried away. Have you had a medical recently?"

****

Dotty sat on her bed and lifted the lid of a dusty
hatbox she'd removed from the top of the wardrobe.
She'd assured Nigel that a medical check was
unnecessary. She was remarkably healthy and
rarely had cause to consult a doctor in her entire
married life; at least not for the usual reasons;
although she hadn't admitted this to Nigel.

A number of visits she'd made to the surgery over
the years had been for an entirely different purpose;
the proof of which was to be found inside a plain
brown envelope hidden beneath family mementoes.

Carefully, as if partaking in a familiar ritual, Dotty
removed all those poignant reminders of family
life: her children's faded christening cards, creased
first school reports, the lucky silver horseshoe she'd
carried with her wedding bouquet, and the bride
and groom from the cake with its grubby sliver of
icing still attached, until only the brown envelope
remained in the box.

She picked up the envelope and withdrew her
shiny, unused passport. She couldn't recall now
why she had secretly applied for one a few years
after she'd married Ronald: a subconscious
rebellion against Bournemouth? The secret
knowledge that whatever the confines of her

married life, she held a key to the gateway of a wider world?

Every ten years she'd collected a renewal form from the post office, sat in the photographic booth at the railway station before confronting the passing of the years as she compared the old photograph with the new, and then called at the surgery so the doctor could endorse it; his signature proof that a pillar of the community vouched for her integrity. Bureaucratic nonsense, thought Dotty, I could have been a secret meths drinker for all he knew.

And each time, before slipping her old passport into the envelope, she'd turned its pristine pages, untouched by smudged stamps commemorating visits to Paris, Rome or Monte Carlo, and wondered why she bothered. But who knew what might happen. The girls were growing up now. What if they were to go abroad on a school trip and were taken ill? She might have to fly out at a moment's notice. A couple of renewals later, Richard, her grandson, was starting school. Forget dreams of dining on a candle-lit terrace beneath a star-filled Mediterranean sky. If you loved your family, feared for their safety, a passport was a practical necessity, not a talisman. Oh all right then, she acknowledged, be honest. It was both.

————————

CHAPTER FOUR

On the Sunday following Dotty's visit to Painless Travel the family came to lunch. Since her father's death, Angela had noted with concern the increasing untidiness of the house and the sadly neglected state into which the garden had fallen. Although Jenny seemed oblivious to such changes, Angela and Paul had tried, on a number of occasions, to bring the matter up with Dotty, but she refused to be drawn. The house was much too large for a widow and, as Paul had said, paying someone to maintain the extensive garden to Ronald's previously exacting standards was out of the question. The first priority was to persuade Dotty to sell the house and move into a manageable apartment somewhere close by. When the house was put on the market would be the time to smarten the property up - both inside and out - in readiness for prospective purchasers.

Dotty brought in a roast turkey on a platter and plonked it down in front of Paul.

"Why has this bird only got one leg?" he asked, looking critically at the turkey.

"Special offer at the supermarket," said Dotty.

"Since when have they offered mutilated birds?" asked Paul.

"Who knows," replied Dotty, seating herself at

the other end of the table. "Perhaps it was in a fight."

Paul pulled out the giblets still in their polythene bag. "It certainly has all its giblets," he said with fastidious distaste. "They're still wrapped."

"So they are," said Dotty, unperturbed. "In that case," she added, peering into the gravy boat, "whatever did I boil up for the gravy?"

Angela stared out of the window. Weeds were sprouting thickly in the drive. How her father would have hated that. Something would have to be done.

"We're going to have to talk about your future, Mum," she said.

Damn, thought Dotty, feeling a flutter of apprehension. She'd intended to break her momentous news to the family at the end of the meal. Knowing it would be greeted with less than enthusiasm, she'd hoped a few glasses of wine would put them in a mellower frame of mind. But she couldn't very well stall now.

"It's all organised," she said, spooning vegetables onto a plate and passing it across to Richard. "Nick sold the house without even advertising it."

There was a stunned silence.

"You can't. You can't do this," wailed Jenny.

"Oh but I can and I have," said Dotty. "Even before your father died I was a grass widow. This house is much too big for me on my own."

"Nick didn't say anything to *me* about this," said Jenny. "What a sneaky..."

"That's because I told him I wanted to give you the news when I was good and ready."

"So that's why he wasn't invited to lunch today," retorted a now furious Jenny.

"Exactly," said Dotty, "I didn't want you making a scene."

"I do think," said Paul, in hurt tones, "that you should have consulted me first."

"It's my house," said Dotty, rather rudely.

"But I could have advised you on the price. You've probably...."

"I've done very well, thank you very much," replied Dotty, butting in.

"We'll help you to find a pleasant little flat around here," said Angela, interrupting what she feared might turn into a nasty argument. Surprised by her mother's announcement, nevertheless she was relieved that she had made a sensible decision and the matter was settled.

"I'll worry about that when I get back. I'm going on a trip," said Dotty, pouring gravy onto her turkey.

"It'll do you good to get away for a week or so," said Angela. Really, her mother was being extraordinarily sensible all of a sudden. She'd always assumed that her father had made all the decisions because Dotty was so easily distracted. Perhaps she'd simply never been given the opportunity. "You could go to Bournemouth."

"I most certainly am not going to Bournemouth," said Dotty. "For over forty years your father insisted we went to Bournemouth. I'm sick of it. I'm going abroad."

There was another stunned silence.

"Perhaps if you were to take one of those senior citizen packages with a tour guide you might stay out of trouble," said Paul, sounding far from convinced.

"I'm not going to be sent off like a flippin' parcel," said Dotty, spluttering over a sprout. She swallowed rapidly then, relishing the moment, "I'm going on a grand tour of Europe: Italy, France, Germany, Spain...." She paused, drowned out by the howls of protest her revelation had provoked, and secretly relieved she'd been interrupted: she couldn't remember the names of all the countries she'd booked to visit.

"You will do no such thing!" screamed Jenny in a fury.

"Wow, Gran. Can I come?" asked Richard, gazing at his grandmother with open admiration.

"It's *may'* I come, Richard, "corrected Paul, "and no, you certainly may not."

Dotty turned to Richard. "Perhaps you can join me in a few months' time."

"Months? Months? What are you talking about?" wailed Jenny, choking on a piece of turkey and slamming down her knife and fork.

They look like something out of a Victorian melodrama, thought Dotty as she glanced around the table. The frozen expressions brought back vivid memories of the toy theatre she'd had as a child; its cardboard cut-out characters each depicting a single emotion: Paul, horror; Angela, concern; Richard, delight. And Jenny? Wide-eyed fury. Dotty hadn't enjoyed herself so much for years.

"I think," said Paul, "that you're suffering from delayed shock. We should have expected this. You've been very brave in your own peculiar way."

"Ronald's death is the *reason* I can do it," replied Dotty in some exasperation. "You know he'd never go abroad. The hours I've spent each year at Bournemouth gazing out across the English Channel, longing to see what was on the other side. Through no fault of my own, I'm insular."

"So what," muttered Jenny.."

"Of course I've enjoyed looking after my family," said Dotty, ignoring her. "I'm not complaining. But at last I'm free to do what *I* want to do, and I'm going to do it."

"You don't speak any foreign languages, Mum," said Angela, floundering.

"Since when has that ever stopped the English from going abroad?" retorted Dotty.

Paul wiped his mouth carefully with his napkin and assumed a sickly sweet placatory expression. Now what's coming, wondered Dotty.

"You are the mother of my wife. You are the much-loved grandmother of our son. You are..."

"I'm glad you've finally got that sorted out," said Dotty with unnecessary sarcasm, nonchalantly spearing a carrot.

"I mean I feel a deep sense of responsibility for your well-being. As head of the family now that Ronald's gone, I..."

"Don't worry," interrupted Dotty, "I'm not going to spend all the money from the sale of the house. There'll still be plenty of it left when I join Ronald and his heavenly cucumbers."

Dotty saw the hurt in Paul's eyes and immediately regretted her words. Pompous he may be. Greedy he certainly was not. She knew he was genuinely concerned.

"You can't even get to the supermarket without posting your shopping list on the way," said Jenny. "How will you cope with tickets, passport, Euros? This is madness. You could be mugged."

"I'm more likely to be mugged on my own

doorstep. The Continentals have much greater respect for the old. Anyway," added Dotty hurriedly, realising that 'old' wouldn't help her case, "I'm not old. I'm far from past it. In fact I'm ready for it."

"If you have any problems Gran, I'll come and rescue you," said Richard, clearly hoping she would.

"Don't even think about it, Richard," said Paul.

Jenny pushed her plate away from her in a gesture which Dotty had seen more times than she cared to remember. Her younger daughter was now thirty-three, yet she was wearing the same tight-lipped I-am-being-badly-done-by expression she'd worn in her high chair.

"You'll lose your luggage," said Jenny. "You lose *everything.* You once told me you'd left me in my pram outside Woolworths and didn't remember until you got home."

"Did I? I'd forgotten that," replied Dotty, mildly. She looked at Jenny. "Trust *you* to remember."

"I do think a trip like this is perhaps a bit too ambitious," said Angela.

"What do you suggest I do? Spend the rest of my life buying meals for one in the supermarket? Stuff flipping marrows for the harvest festival? I don't want to say 'If only' before I die. I am ready for Europe."

"But is Europe ready for you?" asked Paul.

"I admit," said Dotty, "that there are those who think I might be a bit impulsive, perhaps even forgetful, but I've brought up a family haven't I? I've got to this age without coming to grief."

"You're the only woman I know who lost her No Claims Bonus in her own drive," said Paul.

"No-one told *me* Ronald's new greenhouse had been delivered," retorted Dotty, winking at Richard who was trying to suppress a smile at his memory of the devastation she had caused.

"We're not criticising you, Mum," said Angela. "We love you. But you've never been abroad before, as you say. This is a huge undertaking. We're concerned, that's all."

It's ironic, thought Dotty, deeply touched. All those years when Angela and Jenny were growing up I was the one warning them of danger. Don't do this. Be careful of that. Don't talk to strangers. Now the roles are reversed. She felt a sudden pang of sympathy for her children. How many times when they'd planned some little adventure had she warned them against it; suggested that they play in the garden. However distracted she might have been, whatever risks she thoughtlessly took herself, the security of her children came first. Well, apart from the time she'd left Jenny outside Woolworths - if indeed she had! She wouldn't put it past Jenny to have made it up.

"So," said Jenny, near to tears. "Now Dad's gone you're going to dump everything that went with your life before."

"I shall take him with me," said Dotty.

Paul, hit by a vision of a coffin in the guard's van, paled visibly. "I hope you don't mean...."

"I shall share my trip with Ronald in my heart. The only way I could share it with him. He'd never have gone bodily."

"You can't go and that's that," said Jenny.

"I can and I will," retorted Dotty.

"You have no right to sell my home and leave the country."

"*Your* home? You've got your own home."

"My divorcee's executive studio? You're threatening my stability. The one fixed point in my life. Whatever's happened to me, you and Dad have always been here. Dad's gone and now you're going. Mothers aren't supposed to bugger off. It's irresponsible."

There was a strained silence at the table. Jenny, embarrassed by her outburst, stared morosely at the tablecloth. Richard idly pushed a piece of turkey around his plate.

Dotty took a deep breath. "I've been a slave to this house all my adult life. We couldn't afford help but your father refused to move to a more manageable place because of his garden. Now it's worth a small fortune. I see the money from its sale as his final gift to me. The freedom and opportunity to...to...bugger off as you put it."

Standing up, Dotty held out her hands. The others silently passed their plates to her. No one else rose. She went into the kitchen.

Paul cleared his throat. "If this madness of your mother's catches on," he said once Dotty was out of earshot, "public transport in Europe is going to be over-run by geriatric delinquents."

Dotty's head appeared, framed in the dining-room hatch. "I would thank you *not* to refer to me as a geriatric delinquent, Paul Pemberton," she said, "or you're in danger of not getting any pudding."

Picking up the oven gloves, Dotty turned to stare out of the kitchen window, her eyes suddenly filling with tears. Pudding, always damned pudding, she thought. I'm pathetic. Thanks to me, Ronald didn't get any before he died. Now I'm threatening my son-in-law with withholding his. It's high time I pulled myself together.

Richard came into the kitchen carrying a couple of vegetable tureens. Seeing his grandmother's doleful expression, he placed them gently on the draining board then turned and wrapped his arms around her, hugging her tightly.

"Cheer up, Gran," he whispered. "You're going to have a fantastic time."

"I certainly am," said Dotty, as Richard released her. She reached down and opened the oven door.

Seconds later, with a grinning Richard beside her, she poked her head once more through the dining-room hatch.

"No one's getting any pudding," she said, "I forgot to put it in the oven."

CHAPTER FIVE

"So," said Dotty, unable to keep the satisfaction out of her voice, "that's the plan. I leave for Europe on Thursday."

It was Monday afternoon and she was in St. Botolph's church hall helping Margaret to sort second-hand clothes for the annual church bring and buy sale. She still found it hard to believe that instead of being stuck behind a stall in a stuffy hall on Saturday as she had been on so many previous years, she'd be in Italy.

The vicar, who'd been hovering around getting in the way as usual, cleared his throat. "I do think such an extended period of travel is precipitously rash," he said. "Who will do the flowers in church each Saturday? Who will help our dear Margaret with the harvest festival supper?"

Not me, thought Dotty. Those days are over. "'The desire accomplished is sweet to the soul,'" she said. "Proverbs, 19."

"'The younger son gathered all together and took his journey into a far country and there wasted his substance on riotous living,'" countered the vicar. "St. Luke."

Oh for some riotous living, thought Dotty, but she only said "I'll arrange for my weekly donations to the church to continue in my absence."

"That is most gratifying, thank you so much," said the vicar wandering off and leaving Dotty to ponder the meaning of Christian charity. All the years she'd helped St. Botolph's, and the vicar could only think about the church coffers and the inconvenience her absence would cause him. Strange how vicars were always so obsessed with money. *They* obviously didn't believe in the maxim 'God will provide'. Still, in fairness, she was being selfish, doing what *she* wanted to do. But then, after waiting so long, why not, now she had the opportunity? The vicar could at least have wished her Godspeed.

Dotty glanced furtively at Margaret, who had remained silent. She was folding a sweater with studied care. For once, thought Dotty, I've finally rendered her speechless. When was she going to say: 'I wouldn't do that, dear, if I were you?'"

Margaret placed the sweater on top of a pile of other clothes. "It's not going to be easy," she said, "but I'm prepared, just for your sake, to leave Tomkins with my sister for a while."

"What?" said Dotty rudely, startled.

"My cat, dear. I've decided to come with you. You can't possibly go around Europe for months on your own. You know how disorganised you are. If you're determined to take off like this, I feel it my duty to come with you. What are friends for?"

Dotty was so astonished she could only manage another "What?"

"I don't want you to think that now you've sold the house...I mean I shall, of course, pay my own way. I do have some savings."

"Oh no," said Dotty, "I mean, thank you Margaret, it's very thoughtful of you, but you can't possibly leave Tomkins and you mustn't even think about your savings and..." Embarrassed by the turn the conversation had taken, Dotty realised she was babbling.

"Don't you want to share the experience?" asked Margaret somewhat plaintively.

"It's human nature to want to share," replied Dotty, "to imagine sitting contentedly beside a kindred spirit watching a perfect sunset. But other people never do sit contentedly, do they? They usually say 'My bottom's gone numb' or 'Do you think we could find a drink around here?' And spoil it."

"You know I don't drink, dear," said Margaret.

"What about your painful bunions?" Dotty asked, clutching desperately at straws.

"They have chiropodists in Europe, dear," replied Margaret. "Foreigners don't have perfect feet either."

"I appreciate your concern," said Dotty, "I really do, but this is *my* adventure."

"I suppose it is," said Margaret, sounding bitterly disappointed. "It was just that I suddenly realised, when you told me about your plans, that perhaps you were right to do something a bit different before it was too late."

Dotty left the church hall, deep in thought; upset by Margaret's offer to accompany her and equally upset that she'd found herself unable to accept it. Margaret the cautious. Margaret the organised. Who would have believed it. It was extraordinary how her decision to go abroad had provoked her family and friends into revealing a side of themselves she'd never have suspected. How many of us pretend we're happy with what we've got; resign ourselves, usually with a good grace, to the certain knowledge that fantasies will remain forever unfulfilled? Margaret would never have considered making such a journey alone, but if someone else acted as a catalyst, gave her the courage, she'd go along for the ride.

But not with me, thought Dotty. It had been very difficult to explain to Margaret, without hurting her feelings, why she wanted to go alone, particularly when, not having expected such an offer, she'd been forced to clarify on the hoof her reasons for refusing it. Margaret's presence would change everything; her needs would have to be taken into consideration. For a start, her feet would preclude any extended periods of sightseeing. And even if she went off alone to explore leaving Margaret to sit and watch the world go by, she'd have to tell her what time she would return, punctuate her wanderings with glances at her watch. Not out of simply courtesy either. She'd only have to be ten minutes late and Margaret would be alerting Interpol.

She'd always put her family's needs first. This Grand Tour was an opportunity to consider her own. But in order to do so, she'd hurt the feelings of a good friend. I haven't left home yet, thought Dotty, bemused, and I've learned more in the past few weeks about myself and those around me than I've learned in years. Travel certainly does broaden the mind.

Dotty was still preoccupied with her thoughts when she walked into Painless Travel and found Nigel concentrating fiercely on his computer. She moved quietly across the room so as not to disturb him and sank into a chair, suddenly feeling very weary.

Nigel looked up from his computer and noted her solemn expression. "You've changed your mind, haven't you.," he said, clearly pleased.

Dotty shook her head.

Nigel sighed, and reaching down into a desk

drawer pulled out a large brown envelope. He tipped the contents onto his desk and then, picking up each item one by one, placed them directly in front of Dotty.

"Airline ticket, rail tickets, hotel reservations, list of Euro cheque numbers to be kept separate for when, I mean if you get mugged. Insurance policy. List of all-night chemists and hospital emergency numbers in Italy. I'll send you the next lot before you go on to Spain. My telephone and fax numbers and e-mail address."

Dotty stared at the pile of documents. "Good Heavens. I need all this?"

Nigel slammed his hand down on top of them. "You're quite sure you don't want to change your mind?"

"Positive," said Dotty, standing up and sweeping everything into her shopping bag.

"You're a brave, but foolhardy woman, Mrs Lucas."

Dotty's mood suddenly lightened as she thought of what lay ahead of her. "Just think, Nigel," she said, "In three days I shall be stepping out into the great unknown."

Nigel gave a terrified little whimper. "No, no, Mrs Lucas. You'll be going where Nigel sends you, so long as you remember my motto which is?"

Dotty dropped her shopping bag. "Stick to the

schedule. Don't tamper with the timetable. And stay…on….the...rails," she sang, doing a little jig.

"Otherwise," said Nigel, somewhat taken aback, "I won't be able to cope. And then where would you be?"

"Up the Orinoco without a paddle," said Dotty.

"Please, Mrs Lucas. Don't even think about the Orinoco."

Dotty picked up her bag and leaning impulsively across the desk gave Nigel a big kiss on his cheek. "Thank you for everything," she said, "I won't come to any harm."

"You will if you go around kissing people you hardly know," he replied, whipping off his glasses and polishing them furiously to hide his embarrassment.

"Goodbye, Nigel," she said. "I'll keep in touch."

"And stay away from foreigners," he yelled as she was about to close the door behind her. "They're all mad."

****

On Wednesday evening Jenny, Angela and Paul were in Dotty's sitting room, assembling the luggage for her trip. Dotty, coming in from the kitchen where she'd been preparing dinner for them all, was aghast at the enormous pile.

"What if I decide to go to Venice," she said sarcastically, "you've forgotten to pack a gondola. I'm not taking all this lot."

"We thought you should be well prepared," said Angela.

Dotty lifted a large suitcase with considerable difficulty. "What's in here? Your father?"

"A well-stocked first aid kit," said Jenny, "in case of an emergency."

"The first emergency will be a hernia before I've even got on the plane," replied Dotty ungraciously, dumping the suitcase to one side. She picked up three umbrellas and brandished them threateningly. "And these?"

"You know perfectly well you always lose them," said Jenny. "So I've packed a couple of spares."

Dotty chucked the umbrellas onto her growing discard pile. "I want to feel foreign rain on my face."

"It's wet," said Paul, "like ours. Probably wetter."

Snatching up a dress from an open suitcase Dotty peered at the label. "Name tapes?" She turned to Jenny. "With *your* telephone number?"

"We always had them in our school knickers," said Jenny, looking hurt that her thoughtful gesture had not been appreciated.

"Not in those as well." said Dotty, horrified, rooting through her other clothes.

"Your solicitors do have it in writing that the new owner doesn't wish to move in for at least three months?" asked Paul.

"We've agreed I can leave the house exactly as it is for now," replied Dotty, continuing to chuck things onto the discard pile while uncomfortably aware that her reply gave credence to Paul's assumption that the house had been sold with delayed possession and the money from the sale was safely in the bank. The truth was somewhat different, but she wasn't going to worry about that now.

She picked up a strange object and held it aloft. "What's this? A gun holster for Pistol Packing Mama?"

"It's a money belt," said Angela. "You wear it around your waist."

"Thank you," said Dotty. "It's nice to know my family's finally done something sensible for once."

A couple of hours later Dotty and Angela were alone in the sitting room. There was now a single suitcase and a small travelling case by the door. Dotty was proudly wearing her money belt, enjoying the novelty of it.

"That's that then," she said, "travelling light."

"Oh Mum," said Angela, "I don't want you to go but a small part of me envies you."

"Nothing wrong between you and Paul is there?

He's a bit pompous like all civil servants, but he does love you. He's a good man."

Angela smiled. "We're fine," she said. "It's just that…well…it's exciting to be doing something different like this…to wander as you please."

"And I'm only free to do it because I've lost your father. I do miss him, you know. Carrying on as before - but without him - could never be the same."

"I think, in his way, he'd have been very proud of you," said Angela.

Early the following morning Dotty knelt beside Ronald's grave admiring the headstone:

Ronald Lucas
Loving Husband, Father, and Grandfather
Aged 72 Years
A Man who Knew his Onions

The church authorities had initially baulked at the last line but the vicar had talked them into agreeing. All those pickles and preserves she'd made and sold on behalf of the church must have tipped the balance.

"Well, Ronald," said Dotty softly. "In three hours I'll be on my way to Europe. I'm very excited - and a bit nervous, but I'm not going to let the family see. Look after yourself while I'm away. *Au revoir! Auf Wiedersehen! Arriverderci!* Pretty good eh? At least it's a start."

Hearing footsteps, she looked up and saw Nick approaching, dressed in a black suit, white shirt and black tie.

"Hello, Nick," said Dotty, rising to her feet. "I saw there was a funeral today. Going to check up on whether the relatives want to sell the house?"

Nick, for once, looked embarrassed.

"Can't see anything wrong in being first off the mark," she continued. "If you hadn't sold *my* house so quickly I wouldn't be leaving for Europe today."

There was no response from Nick whose attention was firmly fixed on the artistic arrangement of leafy topped carrots, celery and parsley which filled the flower vase on Ronald's grave.

"I thought it would make Ronald feel at home," said Dotty.

CHAPTER SIX

The family accompanied Dotty to the airport, not only from an understandable desire to prolong the moment before they had to say their farewells, but also from an equally understandable concern that she and her travel documents arrived simultaneously at the check-in desk. What happened after that, they inwardly acknowledged with varying degrees of apprehension, was outside their control. Richard's request that they should then go up to the viewing deck to watch the plane take off was quashed by his father, who had a sudden, nightmarish vision of his mother-in-law standing on a wing, waving madly as the plane rose into the sky, like that actress whose name he couldn't remember in the film *Flying Down to Rio.*

"Oh Mum," wailed a tearful Jenny, "what am I going to do without you?"

"You'll manage," said Dotty firmly.

Angela hugged her mother. "Have a wonderful time. I'll be thinking of you. Stay in touch."

"My travel agent, Nigel, will always know where I am, even if I don't," said Dotty.

Paul, doubting the likelihood that Nigel had psychic powers, kissed his mother-in-law on the cheek. "Please," he begged her, "do try to keep a low profile; a very low profile. I have a promotion coming up next month."

Richard, who had carried his grandmother's luggage over to the check-in desk, lifted her off her feet, holding her close. "Don't forget what I taught you about defending yourself," he whispered in her ear.

"*What* did you teach your grandmother?" asked Paul suspiciously.

"Oh nothing you need to worry about," Dotty replied, as she and Richard exchanged conspiratorial glances.

Much as she loved her family she was impatient for them to leave, eager to savour alone the excitement of being in an airport for the first time; to take her place in the cosmopolitan world of jet setters. She was also keen to see the back of Jenny. Unworthy as her unease might be, she had a sneaky fear that her younger daughter would suddenly produce a suitcase of her own and whisper "Surprise, Surprise!"

The family was about to leave the concourse when Richard lifted his camera.

"Ready Gran? One more for the album," he called.

Dotty whipped open her jacket to reveal a white T-shirt with *Granny Takes Off* emblazoned across the front.

"Oh Richard, how could you!" groaned Paul, fortunately unaware that the word *Everything* was printed across the back.

At - long last. *This* is the moment I've been waiting for, exulted Dotty, handing over her passport with a flourish, before experiencing a twinge of childish disappointment when the official barely glanced at it. But then, what had she expected? - A red carpet and brass band? Once through baggage check, stepping into the enclosed, enticing world of duty-free shops, she paused for a moment, fighting against her innate curiosity. Determined on this occasion not to allow herself to be distracted and risk missing her plane, she forced her attention on the bewildering plethora of directional signs. Locating her gate number, she set off purposefully on the long trek to the departure lounge, just as another Dorothy before her had followed the yellow brick road.

Waiting impatiently for her flight to be called, she regarded her fellow passengers with scorn, the majority of whom were talking on mobile phones.

What was the matter with people, she wondered, with their constant desire to stay in touch with those left behind rather than looking forward to what lay ahead. Jenny, having tried to persuade her mother to take a mobile phone on her travels, had sulked when she'd vehemently refused. The last thing she wanted was a succession of mournful enquiries from her younger daughter: "Where are you now? What are you doing?" and inevitably "When are you coming back?"

Oh sod Friends of the Earth, thought Dotty with environmental disdain, as she was unexpectedly but blissfully assailed by the cloying and comforting smell of kerosene while crossing the tarmac to the waiting plane. How incongruous that minutes before the jet headed for the skies, she should be transported back so vividly to winter nights in her childhood bedroom; lying in a warm fug, lulled to sleep by the soporific flickering patterns thrown up on the ceiling by the paraffin stove. Her father would tiptoe in to remove the stove when he came to bed.

Clambering up the steep steps to board the aircraft, she was overwhelmed by the sheer size of it towering above her. Reaching the top step, intoxicated by the drama of this historic moment, she halted abruptly. Ignoring the bunched-up consternation of passengers following behind, she turned back and gazing out across the tarmac, raised her arm high in graceful salute as so many departing dignitaries had done before her, then whipped around and stepped smartly on to the plane.

Safely installed in her window seat, watching, in fascination as passengers continued to pour down the aisle, she felt illogically reassured by the presence of half a dozen dog-collared priests: smooth shaven, shiny-cheeked young men with horn-rimmed glasses magnifying innocent eyes. Taking off on a wing and a prayer was all very well, but some serious professional help in getting this metal monster off the ground certainly wouldn't go amiss.

Dotty was glancing at the safety instruction sheet when a diminutive elderly lady with beautiful snow-white hair and sun-tanned face the texture of a walnut shell, slipped into the aisle seat and promptly fastened her seat-belt with the relaxed, practised air of a seasoned flyer.

"See that little whistle on the life jacket?" she said, pointing scornfully at a colourful diagram. "You're supposed to blow that to attract attention if the plane crashes. Fat lot of help if you've belly flopped into 20-foot waves in the middle of the Atlantic Ocean. I ask you. Sorry love," she added, seeing Dotty blink nervously, "I didn't mean to scare you. I'm Nelly Broadbent."

"Dorothy Lucas. I'm not remotely scared," replied Dotty sharply, irritated by Nelly's condescension. "And," she continued, swiftly comparing her own robustly healthy body with the little stick insect beside her, "I'm a very strong swimmer. And you?"

"Like a fish," Nelly shot back triumphantly. "Fly often, do you?" she persisted, sensing Dotty's defensiveness.

"I prefer to travel by boat and train," Dotty replied, "You see more."

"Where've you been then?"

Dotty shrugged. "Oh all over," she said, making an airy gesture indicating the world was her oyster. Fearing Nelly would ask her to be more specific and expose her lack of sophistication, she hurried on: "Italy's just the first stop on *this* trip. I'm touring Europe for a few months. Spain, France, Switzerland... wherever my fancy takes me really." That should be sufficient proof of my travelling credentials, she thought, underestimating her fellow passenger.

"It would make more sense to start in France and work your way down rather than shunting backwards and forwards," Nelly chipped in, irritating Dotty even more.

"I thought a few weeks' relaxing at a health spa would be an ideal way to prepare for such an extended tour. A bit of pampering, massage...you know the sort of thing," said Dotty, hoping she didn't.

"Mud baths and monkey gland injections. Not my cup of tea," said Nelly. "Tried one in Brazil a couple of years back. Bored out of my mind after three days."

Punch drunk from slugging it out with this combative whippet, Dotty reached down and lifted her travelling case. Opening it on her lap, she pointedly removed her Sony Walkman and Italian language tape. A framed photograph of Ronald holding a giant cucumber was slotted into the lid of the case.

"Blimey," said Nelly, appreciatively, "He's got a whopper."

Dotty closed the case and slipped it back under the seat in front of her. "Gold Cup winner five years running," she murmured smugly, slipping on her headphones.

As the plane began to taxi out, Dotty removed her headphones, her eyes glued to the window. An expectant hush descended upon the cabin as the plane paused at the beginning of the runway, rocking slightly, transmitting a palpable sense of contained energy hovering on the edge of release. Birds do it all the time, she told herself, feeling the physical force of the acceleration as the jet hammered down the runway.

She held her breath. As the tarmac receded and the plane seemed to hang suspended before surging upwards she experienced a joyful sense of liberation.

"Soon be at 26 thousand feet," said Nelly nonchalantly, miffed to see that rather than being unnerved by her remark, as she'd intended, her travelling companion simply smiled happily, clearly delighted.

If Ronald was looking down from Heaven, they'd be closer than they'd been for some time.

When the stewardess handed them their lunch trays

Nelly removed her lid and placed it on the table in front of the empty seat between them. As Dotty followed suit, she turned slightly and saw Nelly, who'd been fumbling in her handbag, whip out her hand, push something rapidly into her rice and chicken, and with an agonised scream slump forward in an apparent faint.

As passengers turned around in their seats and a stewardess raced down the aisle towards them, Dotty stared in open-mouthed astonishment at what, if a protruding tail was anything to go by, looked like the decomposed remains of a mouse.

Nelly slowly raised her head as the stewardess appeared beside her. "There's...there's...something. in...in…my..." she whimpered, pointing at her lunch tray.

The stewardess glanced down. With a gasp of horror she snatched the tray away and, covering her mouth with her other hand, ran to the galley. Nelly, her eyes closed, continued to moan softly as Dotty, still rigid with shock, gazed unseeing at the back of the seat in front of her.

The stewardess returned clutching another food tray and a bottle. "I'm so sorry," she whispered, placing them on the table in front of Nelly, "I've brought you a fillet steak from Club Class and a small bottle of champagne with our compliments."

Nelly looked up with a brave expression on her

pinched little face. "I didn't mean to make such a fuss, love," she said soothingly, patting the stewardess's hand. "These things happen. Don't give it another thought."

"No, no, it's terrible," the stewardess whispered in her ear. "When we land you must go to the desk clerk. We'll give you a voucher for a free return ticket. I am so sorry."

"Oh I couldn't possibly accept," said Nelly.

"No, please, you must!" The stewardess looked across at Dotty, who was still wearing her look of frozen astonishment. "And your friend. She is upset. She will have a free ticket one-way. We mustn't spoil your holiday."

Nelly smiled graciously. The stewardess, relieved, walked back down the plane. Nelly turned her head slowly and looked warily at Dotty.

"You...you..." began Dotty.

"You saw me..."

Dotty nodded.

"*You've* got a free ticket as well," Nelly hissed, giving her a fierce look.

"I couldn't possibly accept," said Dotty, mimicking her words to the stewardess.

"Much cheaper for them than being sued," said Nelly. "Anyway, they'll only be filling an empty seat. The flight I took to Hong Kong was half empty. And if I hadn't flown with a voucher to Bermuda there'd have been no one on but the crew."

"You do this all the time?" asked Dotty

"I couldn't get further than the corner shop on my pension," replied Nelly, attacking her fillet steak with obvious appreciation.

"But that's not the impression you give!" Dotty indicated Nelly's elegant suit and jewellery; so understated she was sure they must be expensive.

"They'd be suspicious if you looked as if you *needed* to do it," replied Nelly.

Dotty remained silent, staring at the sauce congealing on her bit of chicken, her appetite lost, her mind whirling. Nelly, registering her companion's confusion, instinctively responded in the time honoured way of petty crooks with a show of bravado, inviting complicity rather than expressing remorse. Putting down her knife and fork, she reached into her handbag and took out a couple of matchboxes. Shielding them with her body from the passengers across the aisle, she exposed the contents to Dotty.

"This one's blowflies and caterpillars. For restaurants," said Nelly eagerly. "They don't like little old ladies keeling over with shock in the seafood salad. It's bad for business. And these are bugs," she went on, tapping the other box, "For hotel beds. I put them between the sheets. Never fails." She dropped the boxes back into her handbag and placed it on the seat between them. "Trouble is, I have to keep on the move a bit sharpish. No going back a second time. And I'm running out of airlines; too many of them going bust at the moment for my liking. And as for those budget operators, well, it's a disgrace," she said with righteous indignation. "They don't feed you."

There was still no response from Dotty. "It's alright for *you*," said Nelly defensively, "You're a Whoopie."

"A what?" asked Dotty.

"One of those Well Off Older People. I'm just a Wrinklie. You want to see the world. Why shouldn't I?"

If Ronald hadn't left me so well provided for, wondered Dotty, what would *I* have done if my circumstances hadn't allowed me, finally, to travel? Although she could in no way condone what Nelly was doing, nevertheless she felt a perverse kind of sympathy for this tough old bird, with her shrewd shoe-button black eyes and alarming aplomb. "Why are you going to Italy?" she asked.

"I'm Catholic," said Nelly. "I'm very fond of the saints. It's the Feast of Saint Rita this week. There'll be processions and fireworks. I love all that stuff. It does my heart good to see it."

Dotty longed to be a fly on the wall of the Confessional when Nelly told all; for she somehow knew beyond any shadow of doubt that she *would* seek absolution - with the same regularity as she sinned.

Disembarking from the plane, Dotty impulsively went down on all fours and kissed the ground.

"Are you alright?" asked Nelly, fearing she'd taken a tumble.

"I've seen the Pope do it," said Dotty, taking Nelly's proffered hand and rising to her feet.

"*You're* Catholic?"

"Nope," Dotty replied, inelegantly spitting out a piece of grit, "But I know just how he feels."

Nelly gave her an old-fashioned look. "There's more to you than meets the eye, Dorothy," she said.

As the pair emerged from the baggage hall Nelly pointed to the airline desk. "That's where we pick up our vouchers."

Dotty shook her head. "No thanks," she said. Back on *terra firma,* the journey had already taken on a dreamlike quality. Soaring over Europe for the first time, looking down in wonder on the Alps, being an unwilling captive to Nelly's underhand activities seemed now to have occurred in a parallel universe. She was eager to break the connection between them. "Which hotel are you staying at?" she asked warily.

"I'm not. I'm staying with some friends," replied Nelly, sensing it was time to make herself scarce. "It was nice meeting you, Dorothy. Maybe I'll bump into you again -in a restaurant." Giving Dotty a knowing wink, she picked up her suitcase and walked off purposefully in the direction of the airline desk.

Nigel, fearing Dotty might be abducted, had conscientiously arranged for the hotel to send a taxi to meet her. Pushing her way through the jostling crowd emerging from the airport, she scanned the boards held aloft by a motley crowd of meeters and greeters. There it was. *Lucas. Hotel Palladio Terme.* Relieved, she hailed a cloth-capped Italian with a gnarled and kindly face who, with a nod and a smile, took her suitcase and indicated she should follow him.

Nelly was forgotten, blanked out by excitement as the taxi left the airport. Dotty feasted her eyes upon cypress trees that reminded her of shaving brushes, peachy stuccoed villas; cosy little farmhouses set amidst neatly cultivated patches of vines and vegetables surrounded by fields aflame with blood-red poppies and wild flowers in dreamlike profusion. The sun shone from a cloudless turquoise sky.

The taxi driver glanced at her in his mirror, smiling at her rapt expression. He'd seen it so many times before on foreigners arriving in Italy, instantly seduced.

"*Inglese?*" he asked.

"Er...*si,*" replied Dotty with obvious pleasure at understanding his enquiry. Her brows knitted, concentrating fiercely, she enunciated slowly and carefully *"Questa...e...un...paese...bellissimo,"* - this is a beautiful country.

"Grazie tanto," said the taxi driver. Although the *signora's* pronunciation was *terribile,* and the sentiment expressed only to be expected, nevertheless it was always appreciated.

The taxi took a sharp turn off the main road thickly tapestried with trees and the small town of Bellarosa came into view atop a steep hill. Its mellow stone houses with weathered shutters and undulating terracotta tiled roofs rose in a series of steep terraces; the houses leaning drunkenly against one another, as if hoping that such mutual support would save them from sliding into the valley below. Dotty pressed her nose to the window as the taxi snaked its way up to the summit. They entered the town through an impressive ancient gateway and emerged into a cobbled square of timeless sunlit charm. Everything appeared to be under a spell of enchantment.

The streets were deserted except for an old man dozing on a bench, roses cascading down a wall behind him, his walking stick wedged between his knees. Shutters were closed; metal grills pulled down over shop windows. A pock-marked marble Titan crouching uncomfortably in the fountain was only dribbling; as if even he couldn't be bothered to exert himself. The silence was broken by the bell on a crooked church tower at the far end of the *piazza,* tolling the hour.

It's like a scene from *High Noon,* thought Dotty, expecting at any moment to see James Stewart and a stubble-chinned villain emerging from dark alleys at opposite ends of the square, guns pointing at the ready. Where was everybody?

"La siesta," said the taxi driver, noting her bewilderment, and for good measure adding a couple of loud snores.

They skirted a high stone wall on the far side of the town until a pair of imposing gateposts came into view topped by a couple of grizzled stone lions, who, from their malevolently sated expressions, looked as if some poor creature had just provided them with an excellent lunch. Turning in at the gates, the taxi entered a sweeping drive edged with lime trees and came to a stop in front of a flight of stone steps leading to the impressive double entrance doors of a vast wisteria-clad stuccoed villa imbued with all the formidable assurance and arrogance of centuries.

"Eccolo!" said the driver, turning round and grinning at Dotty's open-mouthed astonishment. "Hotel Palladio Terme."

"Good Lord, Ronald," she murmured, as a liveried porter ran down the steps to meet her, "I hope they'll let me in without a tiara."

CHAPTER SEVEN

Floating in a bubble of delight, Dotty barely registered the formalities at the reception desk, where an elegant young man, as handsome as a movie star - his eyelashes the length of spider's legs - introduced himself as Luigi and welcomed her warmly. She wasn't aware of the porter's departure after he'd accompanied her to her room and deposited her luggage, so overcome was she by the luxuriousness of her surroundings.

She gawped at the gleaming tessellated floor, oriental rugs, enormous half-tester bed, walnut wardrobe, chaise longue, and an antique table on which sat a bowl of fresh fruit as artfully arranged as a still life. Wooden shutters framed double glass doors leading on to a small balcony, the wall creeper-clad, the iron balustrade clotted with hanging tubs of scarlet geraniums.

She crossed the room and opened the door to the bathroom. Confronted by half a dozen images of herself in the mirrored walls, she stared in wonderment at the thick white towels stacked on a marble shelf, the fluffy folded bathrobe, hair dryer and basket filled with toiletries beside a washbasin with gleaming taps. Her gaze fell upon a white paper strip stretched across the lavatory lid, bearing the words. *Sanitised for your protection.* Removing the tiny pair of grape scissors from the fruit bowl, she returned to the bathroom.

"It gives me great pleasure," she declaimed in regally dulcet tones as she snipped through the sanitised paper with exaggerated care, "to declare this lavatory open."

****

Richard was in his bedroom, standing in front of a large-scale map of Europe he'd affixed to the wall. He was just about to pin a flag marked *Bellarosa* to it when his father walked in.

"I think it would have been sensible to wait a few days before starting this, Richard," he said, spinning round as Angela rushed in behind him, smiling happily.

"That was Mum on the phone from Italy," she said. "She says she feels as if she's died and gone to Heaven."

"Well that's a relief," said Paul, "Sorry I didn't mean it the way..."

"I know what you meant," said Angela, coming to his rescue. To Richard's obvious enjoyment and Paul's moral indignation, she repeated Dotty's far from censorious account of her meeting with Nelly Broadbent.

"What did I just say?" said Paul to his son. "No

sooner has your grandmother left the country than she's consorting with criminals." He turned to Angela. "Your mother may survive her travels," he said pitifully, "but I'm not sure I shall."

Picking up the *Bellarosa* flag Richard jabbed it firmly into the map. "Good old Gran," he murmured, "She's off and running."

****

Wearing the fluffy hooded towelling robe, her head encased in rollers, Dotty stretched out luxuriously on the bed and fell back against the soft pillows. She'd used the bubble bath and body lotion, eaten most of the fruit, and given herself a stomach ache. She'd also used the hair dryer somewhat sooner than she'd expected. Unfamiliar with the dual-purpose lever on continental bath fittings, she'd reached down to turn on the taps and been hit with considerable force on the head and shoulders by a deluge of spray from the shower. Having stripped off her clothes, mopped the floor with a towel and then wrapped her head in another one, she'd sought solace in a miniature of whisky from the mini-bar before her second, this time successful attempt to run the bath water.

Now, lying on the bed, converting the euro price list into sterling, she felt in need of another stiff drink to numb the shock of what the first one had cost. She hoped everything else was complimentary or she'd be back in Bournemouth the following week, in a boarding-house. Oh, what the heck, she told herself, this is your first day. Enjoy it.

She raised her eyes to the frescoed ceiling, where chubby cherubs with blonde curls and expressions of unbridled mischief were cavorting far from innocently in a sylvan glade with a group of well-endowed maidens. Naked, except for wisps of drapery, the ladies were looking far from pleased at being under attack from a welter of fat little pink hands, which were avidly twiddling their nipples, squeezing their rosy cheeked bottoms and clinging on to their thighs while simultaneously blowing trumpets and plucking peaches from the trees. She presumed there must be some meaning to all of this but she couldn't think what it might be. What she did know was that rather than being indulged, the cherubs deserved a good smack on their own bottoms. In these days of political correctness, they'd be had-up for sexual harassment.

Some picnic, she thought, comparing it with the usually rain-drenched bash the Reverend Henderson arranged each year on the vicarage lawn. It was a good job Margaret hadn't accompanied her on her travels. Dotty giggled, imagining her friend's reaction if this had been the first thing she'd seen when she opened her eyes each morning.

She rose, crossed the room and opened the doors to her balcony. Stepping out, she rested her arms on the railing, shaking her head in wonder at the idyllic scene below. Roses in full bloom sprawled languorously over a pergola. A series of broad-lawn terraces descended a gentle slope flanked by stone balustrades with niches each accommodating an enormous urn containing a lemon tree. At the base of the lawns, clipped box hedges enclosed an arbour with benches encircling a pool overhung with cascading honeysuckle and wisteria.

How Ronald would have loved this, she thought, wishing he were standing beside her. But then, if he had been alive, she wouldn't have been here anyway. He had never appeared to need the stimulation of the new; he was happy pottering at home. Was it simply that he'd been born content, or was his lack of desire to travel a fear of not being in control; vulnerable outside his own safe little patch? Was she so often distracted because she was never satisfied; or just curious by nature and eager to experience all she could before it was too late?

She glanced at her watch. It was time to dress. She mustn't miss her pre-dinner appointment. In a place such as this, she didn't want to start off on the wrong foot. Guests were asked to attend a preliminary consultation with the resident doctor who would advise them, depending upon their state of health, on which spa treatments would be most beneficial.

Dotty felt a flutter of apprehension as she descended the stairs to the reception hall, smoothing the creases from her old cotton dress and   hoping she wouldn't look like the poor relation when she joined the other hotel guests. She recalled the words of a friend's 6 year-old granddaughter who, when asked her philosophy of life, had replied with stunningly precocious common sense: "Do your work day by day. Never worry about a thing. And always wear the right clothes for the right occasion."   In the past, thought Dotty, I've lived by the first two, but not bothered much about the third.

Luigi directed her to the consultation room where she was greeted by a white- coated doctor with soulful brown eyes. She emerged ten minutes later, feeling smug, having been pronounced very healthy and complimented upon her blood pressure reading which, the doctor had informed her, would be the envy of a woman half her age. "No problems," he said. "Just enjoy yourself, *signora.*"

The hotel had woken up after its siesta. Some of her fellow guests were standing in animated groups in the spacious reception hall, others were already seated at tables on the terrace where dinner would be served every evening unless - and this was unlikely,

Luigi had assured her - it turned cold. Casting furtive glances around her, Dotty judged most of the guests to be around her own age, although not all in her state of health. A couple of them were shuffling along with the help of walking sticks. She was relieved to see that although the women were smartly dressed - some more elegant than others - she'd managed to keep her end up and wouldn't let the Queen down!

One of the guests, a handsome, bronzed, silver-haired man, whom she judged to be in his sixties, and who had been conversing rapidly in Italian with Luigi, strode purposefully across the hall. He didn't have a body so much as a broad muscular torso supported by two Italian length legs. He didn't walk, he parted the air.

Drawing level with Dotty he acknowledged her presence with a dignified bow of his head and indicated she should precede him on to the terrace. As the *maitre'd* showed her to her table, her stomach did a quick flip when she saw the Italian taking his seat at the table next to hers. Pull yourself together, she told herself severely, shocked by her reaction. It must be those damned cherubs.

The Italian, eating his spaghetti rapidly, to the manner born, had been surreptitiously watching Dotty, who was fighting a losing battle with her pasta. As she picked up her napkin to wipe the sauce from her chin after another vain attempt to lift more than a few strands to her mouth, he could stand the strain no longer.

"*signora*" he called softly. "Take the fork and push some of the spaghetti to the side of the dish. Then wind the spaghetti round and round until it is all safely on the fork."

Dotty picked up her fork and did as she'd been told.

"*Brava*!" he said. "Now eat!"

Having collected far too much pasta onto her fork, Dotty lifted it to her mouth only to fail yet again. The spaghetti slopped back on to the plate, splashing her dress with tomato sauce. She wiped her mouth once more on her stained napkin as the Italian raised his eyes to heaven.

"Why does it have to be so long?" she asked him in exasperation.

"If it was short," he replied "it would not be spaghetti."

"It would be easier to eat."

"Ah, but then life would be too easy."

To his horror, she picked up her knife and fork and started to cut the spaghetti into small pieces. "We don't have this problem back home," she said. "If you can't be bothered with all this nonsense, you can buy it in tins. When my children were small they loved to eat what they called 'worms on toast'."

The Italian shrugged, as only an Italian can shrug,

with an eloquence that conveyed deep distaste for such an insult to his native cuisine; that such a remark was only to be expected from the philistine English, as well as a tolerant acceptance that everyone had a right to their own opinion however much he might deplore it.

"You speak English very well," said Dotty, now happily making progress with her spaghetti. "How did you know I was English?"

"It was not difficult," the man replied with feeling. "Forgive me for not introducing myself," he added "my name is Roberto Carducci."

"Dorothy Lucas," replied Dotty

"Ah, *Dorothea*" said Roberto, giving the Italian version of her name. "There was a *Santa Dorothea* - Saint Dorothy. She was executed."

"That doesn't surprise me," acknowledged Dotty, "you're unlikely to be made a saint unless you've come to a sticky end. Why was she executed?" she asked, her curiosity aroused by her namesake.

"Because she was a Christian. As she was going to her execution, the Judge's secretary asked her to send him some fruit and roses when she got to Paradise."

"Why?" asked Dotty, gazing around her, "I wouldn't have thought there was a shortage down here."

"Because," continued Roberto, not pleased at being interrupted, "he did not believe there was such a thing as paradiso -Heaven, so he was being sarcastic." He paused as the waiter removed their spaghetti dishes and replaced them with plates of roast veal.

"Immediately after Dorothea's execution, an angel brought him a basket of apples and roses and said, 'These are from Dorothea in Paradise.' Then he vanished. The clerk was now very ashamed for not believing and converted to Christianity *subito* - immediately."

Roberto picked up the wine bottle on his table and before replenishing his own glass, reached across to Dotty's table and replenished hers. Seeing her surprised expression, he nodded at the bottle she'd ordered. "Mine is better. You will like it," he said, brooking no argument. "In paintings, *Santa Dorothea* is always shown with a rose branch in her hand, a wreath of roses on her head, and some roses and fruit beside her."

Dotty took a sip of the wine he'd poured for her. She didn't know much about wine, but he was quite right. This did taste better. Putting her glass down, she stared in surprise at Roberto. Other than the vicar, and he usually got things muddled, she'd never met a man who could talk about saints like that; particularly one who was seemingly so debonair and worldly.

"How do you know all this?" she asked. "Are you a priest in disguise, taking a sneaky week off?"

Roberto laughed. "I was brought up in a good Catholic family," he replied, "We learned all about the saints when we were children. Some things you never forget."

You and Nelly Broadbent both, thought Dotty. How odd that they should have something in common. Before she could consider this further, she was suddenly overwhelmed by a feeling of desolation. The story of Saint Dorothy had unexpectedly triggered vivid memories of being driven home after Ronald's funeral.

. "Do you know," she said, looking across at Roberto, who, to his consternation, saw her eyes filling with tears. "Roses are *my* favourite flowers. And I wanted my husband to come back as an apple."

Roberto nodded gravely, with a sensitive understanding that no further explanation was required. "So," he said, "you are alone."

"Yes," said Dotty.

"So am I," he replied dramatically. "It is sad to be alone."

Dotty paused with a forkful of veal halfway to her mouth, taken aback by this Mediterranean directness. "I'm having a wonderful time," she said briskly, having rapidly recovered her composure. "I'm seeing the world."

"The English have always travelled," Roberto acknowledged, "to get away from England, I suppose.

Italians feel happiest in their own country; their own village."

"How very insular," said Dotty scornfully, piqued by his rude remark about her own country, even though she'd been longing for years to get away from it. "It's exciting to wake up in the morning in a strange place."

"It is sad to wake up to a day alone," he said mournfully, "and now my wife has passed on, there is nobody to do my shirts."

"You can send them to the laundry," replied Dotty with asperity, remembering the many boring hours she'd toiled over an ironing board.

"You cannot iron a collar properly without love," said Roberto, his face suffused with regret.

Later that evening, as Roberto collected his room key from the reception desk, he had a quiet word with Luigi, who, after glancing around to ensure no-one else was about, reached behind him, furtively removed a passport from one of the pigeonholes, and handed it to Roberto. After taking a quick peek inside, Roberto passed it back to Luigi as the pair of them exchanged conspiratorial smiles.

Dotty, in her nightgown, stood on her balcony, breathing in the scented softness of the night air. The full moon, like a child's golden balloon, hung motionless above the gardens, as though tethered by an invisible thread. The stars glittered. Such natural delights fed the soul, but, she wondered, could such beauty ever pall? Could a day arrive when one stopped noticing? Frogs croaked, owls hooted. Peace in the countryside didn't mean an absence of noise but rather sounds that were soothing in the stillness. Wearily content after a perfect day, she took one last lingering look before closing the shutters on the balcony doors.

Even as a child she'd had a sense of being part of a much bigger world than the one she inhabited; and now, as she recalled the all-embracing address she'd scrawled beneath her name on the flyleaf of childhood books, she murmured: "Dorothy Lucas can be contacted at the Hotel Palladio, Bellarosa, Italy, Europe, the World, the Universe..." Spreading her arms wide, she waltzed across the room in a state of unalloyed happiness, and, with a joyful "Yippeeeee" took a flying leap on to the bed.

About to turn off the bedside light, she paused and raised her eyes to the ceiling. "And as for you lot," she said, addressing the lascivious, frolicking cherubs, "I don't think a few hours' kip would go amiss either."

CHAPTER EIGHT

Early the following morning Dotty stepped once more onto her balcony, unable to resist the magnetic pull of the serene landscape that lay beneath her window, silhouetted against a startlingly blue sky. The clarity of the light made her blink. Every blade of dew-drenched grass had an individual brilliance and depth like a cardboard cut-out in a child's pop-up nursery book. Rubbing sleep from her eyes, she felt as if she were still contained in a mysterious and blissful dream, from which she hadn't yet awakened.

She must remember to thank Nigel when they next spoke and apologise for initially pouring scorn on his suggestion that she should start her travels by staying at a spa. In her ignorance, she'd assumed it would be some kind of sanatorium where she'd be subjected to a harsh regime of bottled water, raw carrots and lights out before eight, overseen by bossy harridans in white coats. But when he'd insisted that, if she was hell-bent on taking a mad jaunt across Europe, a couple of weeks of sybaritic pampering would give her a fighting chance of survival, she'd accepted that he might have a point.

Her original doubts resurfaced, however, when she left the splendour of her room and took the tiny lift at one corner of the villa that was used exclusively to descend directly to the entrance of what had once been the stable block and which now contained the treatment rooms. She emerged from the lift into a long and echoing white-tiled passage filled with the clamour of gushing water and lined on both sides with rows of frosted glass doors, the air reeking of sulphur.

White-coated attendants strode towards her swinging buckets filled with steaming mud, before disappearing into the cubicles. On a bench facing her at the end of the corridor sat a row of her fellow guests, who, unrecognisable in their white, hooded robes, looked like monks waiting to be dragged off and martyred on the rack in a Transylvanian horror movie.

As Dotty walked down the corridor doors on either side opened and closed revealing glimpses of a huge man prostrate on a bench encased in a thick layer of baked mud, with only his bald head protruding; and in another, a masseuse kneading and pummelling the flesh of a naked woman as if she were a lump of dough. Thanks very much Nigel, thought Dotty. Welcome to the torture chamber.

Before she had time to take her place beside her fellow victims, a young male attendant popped his head around a door signalling her to join him. Dotty, following him into the white-tiled room, was confronted by an enormous bath into which a thick rubber hosepipe was spewing water. I should have brought a crucifix and a clove of garlic, she thought. Any moment now Boris Karloff's going to walk in, rubbing his hands in glee.

Gianni introduced himself and indicated she should step into the bath. As she slipped off her robe to reveal a swimming costume, he shook his head.

"*Nudo*" he said, grinning. "No clothes."

"I beg your pardon?" said Dotty

"Don't worry," he reassured her. "It is natural."

It may be to you young man, thought Dotty, but it certainly isn't to me. She'd given birth with the help of a midwife, and rarely been examined by a doctor during her entire adult life; even then she'd only had to expose the problem bits of her anatomy to him. No one other than Ronald had ever seen her stark naked. Now she was expected to strip off in front of a young man who looked little older than her grandson. Oh, what the hell. '*When in Rome*' and all that'. She peeled off her swimsuit and stepped into the steaming, bubbling mineral water.

It's a funny old world, she acknowledged ten minutes later, as Gianni played the hoses over her body, the water as soft as silk. I'm enjoying this. It's like being immersed in warm lemonade. There couldn't have been any mention of nudity in the spa's brochure or Nigel would have fainted. And as for Margaret, if she'd survived the shock of the bedroom ceiling, she'd have been carried off on a stretcher after this little episode.

She stepped out of the bath like Venus emerging from the waves and Gianni enveloped her in a big fluffy towel. She dried herself and slipped on her robe. Now nonchalantly swinging her swimsuit from her hand, she was whisked off by Maria into another cubicle, where she clambered happily onto the table to experience her first blissful massage.

Guests were advised to rest for twenty minutes following the treatments, but Maria thoughtfully suggested that as Dotty was her last appointment of the morning, she might prefer to stay where she was and rest on the massage table rather than having to return upstairs to her room. Breakfast was informal and there was no need to get dressed.

So relaxed she wove her way down the passage like a drunk, Dotty headed in the direction of breakfast. A waiter, seeing her searching for her room number on one of the tables, informed her that although guests kept the same table for lunch and dinner, breakfast was informal and guests were permitted to sit wherever they wished.

What larks, she thought, to be in such a luxurious hotel where virtual strangers shared breakfast wearing their towelling robes. Mrs. Worthington at Fawlty Towers in Bournemouth would certainly not have approved of such familiarity.

Many of the tables appeared to be occupied by

married couples - well at least she assumed they must be married because they weren't speaking to one another - but there was an empty chair at the table of an elderly gentlemen wearing tiny rimless spectacles, his face barely visible between a cloud of unruly white hair and a luxuriant white beard. He was reading what looked like a heavy learned journal.

As Dotty joined him, he peered up at her over his spectacles like a benevolent owl and courteously but clumsily rose to his feet, dropping his book and tipping over his chair. Blithely ignoring the confusion as a waiter rushed over to pick them up, he bowed deeply.

"*Guten morgan.*"

"Good morning," said Dotty, as the efficient waiter pulled out a chair for her.

"Johannes Albrecht."

"Dorothy Lucas. I'm English."

"And I am German" he said in English. Seating himself once more he turned to thank the waiter for restoring order.

"*Prego professore,* he replied.

Of course, thought Dotty with delight, he couldn't be anything else but a mad professor.

As the Professor slowly turned the pages of his journal to find his place once more, the waiter returned and placed a jug of coffee, croissants, and small pots of butter and jam on the table.

Dotty stared in disappointment at what passed for a continental breakfast. No wonder Italy had been invaded, she thought; no one would have had the strength to resist before lunch time. Ravenously hungry after her treatments, she moved the cup and saucer towards her, poured coffee and speedily buttered a croissant, oblivious to the Professor, who had lowered his book and was surreptitiously watching her with amusement.

Dotty's eyes rose a fraction above her plate as she scanned the table and spotted what she was searching for beside the Professor's elbow. "Pass the jam, dear," she said, without looking up.

The Professor did as he was asked. As Dotty spread jam on her croissant the waiter returned to the table to ask whether she wanted tea or coffee. Dotty, with her mouth full, looked up at the waiter, then across at the Professor, suddenly aware of what she had done.

"Oh I am sorry," she apologised, colouring with embarrassment, as the waiter left to collect the Professor's breakfast a second time.

"I understand perfectly," said the Professor, kindly putting her at her ease. "This morning I get up and take off my pyjamas and do my toilet and I am deep in thought, so when I return to the bedroom I see my pyjamas which means it must be bedtime and I put them on again and go back to bed. Is there, I am wondering, a different time scale for engrossing thought which can be measured? If it is possible to imagine one has compressed a whole day into half an hour, what effect could this have on the Roman calendar? What effect could it have on simply arriving at the university on time to give my lectures? The implications are enormous."

Dotty was saved from a futile attempt to respond intelligently to a question she couldn't begin to comprehend by a blonde, muscular Valkyrie of indeterminate age. Wearing leather-thonged sandals the size of meat plates and a faded print dress which looked as if it had just emerged from mothballs, she was heading purposefully in their direction preceded by an enormous bosom. To Dotty's amusement, the Professor, who had also spotted her, was trying, with a bathetic lack of success, to make himself invisible.

Greeting the woman in German, he must have made some reference to his table companion, for she replied, with an obvious lack of enthusiasm "Ah English," She turned to Dotty. "Zat is my seat."

"No it isn't," said the Professor with considerable spirit. "Anyone can sit anywhere at breakfast and you were late."

"I am never late," she replied.

The waiter, appearing with the Professor's breakfast tray, placed it on the table and diplomatically brought over an additional chair from a now empty adjacent table.

"I am Helga," she said to Dotty, plonking herself down with a bad grace.

"*Heil.* I mean how do you do. I'm Dorothy Lucas," replied Dotty. She was about to put a spoonful of sugar into her second cup of coffee when Helga's hand shot out and grabbed her wrist.

"No sugar," she said. "It is bad for you."

Dotty slapped Helga's hand away and defiantly added sugar to her coffee. Undeterred, Helga pushed the butter out of her reach. "No more butter," she said. "Animal fat is very dangerous."

The diligent waiter, who must have been wearing a hole in the carpet by now, returned with another tray, fulfilling a no doubt imperiously prearranged dietary requirement. He placed a bowl of muesli and a carton of soya milk on the table. The carton looked vulgarly out of place in the midst of the hotel's elegant china. Dotty assumed it was a deliberate act by the kitchen staff to prove to Helga that it *was* soya and so avoid the inevitable complaint.

"The bowels must move," said Helga earnestly, picking up a spoon. "Nothing must interfere with the movement of the passages. *Das mensch ist, was er isst.*"

"Man is what he eats," translated the Professor for Dotty's benefit, giving her a wink.

"In that case," said Dotty, wrinkling up her nose at the muesli, "I'd rather be sugar and spice and all things nice than sawdust and rabbit droppings."

Helga didn't react. They're all the same these health fanatics, thought Dotty, no sense of humour. Fascinated and repelled by the monstrous Helga and unwilling to conceive of the pair being married, she shot a furtive glance at Helga's hands and saw with relief that she wasn't wearing a wedding ring.

The Professor, reading her thoughts, happily put her out of her misery. "We are fellow academics," he said, "We are part of a group which has come to the villa not only for the treatments but also for a conference on Lepidoptera. The study of butterflies," he explained, seeing Dotty's blank look.

"I am organiser of zis conference," said Helga.

That doesn't surprise me, thought Dotty, bossy old boot. "I love butterflies," she said, "I didn't know you could be an expert in well, just butterflies."

"There are 12,000 different species known to exist," replied the Professor, warming to his subject, "and they are divided into the six most important families. The Swallowtails..."

"But some Swallowtails have no tails," interrupted Helga.

"The Whites..." continued the Professor, ignoring her.

"But many Whites are not white," said Helga, refusing to shut up.

"Blue and Hairstreak butterflies..."

"But many Blues are not blue," said Helga.

"Butterflies can smell, hear, taste and see," said the Professor.

"They taste with their feet," said Helga.

"I've never understood why they weren't called Flutterbys," said Dotty.

"It is a serious subject," replied Helga showing her disapproval of such levity.

Dotty was silent for a moment, then, her face a mask of innocence, she turned to Helga. "I couldn't agree more," she said, "but wouldn't you prefer them to be called anything other than *butter*flies?"

Since her arrival the previous afternoon, there'd been no chance to explore the grounds and buildings adjacent to the villa, but after breakfast Dotty spent a happy hour wandering around, occasionally consulting the booklet giving its history which she'd found on the desk in her bedroom. It was hard to believe, looking at the villa today, in all its glory, that for almost a century it had been left abandoned, neglected and forlorn. The "before" photographs revealed closed, peeling shutters, gaping holes in the roof, once elegant, richly decorated rooms blighted by fungus, their walls stained with damp; the gardens running wild. Now, like a princess roused from her slumbers, it had been restored and cleverly converted, at considerable expense no doubt, to its present-day use.

Dotty peered into a pit from which huge pipes channelled the water, rich in mineral salts and iodine, which gushed from the thermal springs in the bowels of the earth at temperatures reaching 87 degrees. The Ancient Romans, recognising the water's curative benefits, had been the first tourists to the region; they'd even brought their war horses to drink from the pools before battle. The water was mildly radioactive, she read. If I came often enough, she thought, I might glow in the dark.

Beyond the stables and coach houses she came to the private theatre where the Professor had told her the conference would be held. Harking back to the time of the Renaissance when it had been a place of entertainment for the wealthy aristocratic family which had originally owned the villa, it was also being used once again for performances by visiting theatrical troupes. According to a poster pinned to the door, an Italian mime group would be performing there before the conference weekend. Dotty couldn't imagine why any Italians would be *paid* to make extravagant gestures when the entire population seemed to spend much of its time semaphoring madly in all directions. She tried the door, but it was locked. Never mind, she had another treat in store.

She emerged from a wisteria-clad pergola which led to the swimming pool to find many of her fellow guests laid out on sun-beds, soaking up the sun. She spotted the Professor engrossed in his journal, half-hidden in dappled shade beneath the low hanging branches of a chestnut tree; no doubt hoping Helga wouldn't find him.

Roberto was flat on his back, fast asleep beside the pool. Although there was an empty sun-bed beside his, she deliberately moved towards one some distance away. She didn't want to appear forward. In truth, she was feeling somewhat shy of him after their encounter the previous evening; unnerved by the effect his physical presence had had upon her.

A middle-aged woman wearing a flowing kaftan, her hair held back by a matching bandana, looked up at her approach. Bandbox perfect, with nails like blood red talons, she was reading a glossy fashion magazine. Dotty stared in admiration at the cover photograph of a model wearing a midnight blue dress with black lapels, and a jauntily tilted black cocktail hat sporting a couple of peacock feathers and a wisp of a veil.

The woman pushed her gold-rimmed sunglasses down her nose and regarded her over the top of them. Raising her perfectly plucked eyebrows, she registered Dotty's T-shirt, baggy cotton trousers and hair frizzed from her dunking in the mineral bath and, from the expression on her face, didn't like what she saw.

"*Bonjour, Madame,*" she said.

French, thought Dotty, I should have guessed.

"Hello," said Dotty. She pointed at the magazine cover. "Isn't that lovely?"

"You are interested in fashion, *Madame*?" the Frenchwoman enquired in a tone which left no doubt about what Dotty's answer should be.

"Well I ..." began Dotty, riled by her manner.

Madame tapped the photograph with a long nail. "This is designed by Salvatore. He is Italian not French, so it is not quite *haute couture,* but," she shrugged, "it is almost perfection."

"I'm sure Salvatore would be thrilled to know he'd *almost* come up to your exacting standards," said Dotty, with more sarcasm than was advisable in the circumstances.

Thankfully, before Madame could respond, Dotty caught sight of Roberto who had woken up and was signalling for her to join him.

"I saw you with Madame Pompadour," he said, amused by Dotty's thunderous expression as she plonked herself down on the sun-bed beside him, "and thought I should rescue you before there was trouble."

"This place is a proper little United Nations of Europe," said Dotty, "although if Helga and Madame Pompadour are anything to go by, war's going to break out again soon. Is that really the

Frenchwoman's name?" she asked, vague memories stirring of school history lessons.

Roberto shook his head. "It is what the hotel staff call her."

"I seem to be the only English person here," said Dotty.

"And I am the only Italian," said Roberto.

"Isn't that a bit odd?" asked Dotty.

"The English don't like to sit in water every day," said Roberto mischievously, knowing full well her question had been directed at him. "What is that English expression *'Friday night is bath night?'* Sometimes I think it would be better if it was the English who lived in a hot country; there would never be the water shortages we Italians experience."

About to defend her compatriots, Dotty saw Roberto was teasing and refused to rise to the bait.

"Italians go to Montecatini or Chianciano," he continued, "where there is more of a night life. It is mostly Germans who come each year to the spas in this *zona*. They have never stopped invading Italy - but these days it is a peaceful invasion. Instead of taking things away they bring us a lot of money."

"Why don't you go where other Italians go?" asked Dotty.

Roberto grinned. "We Italians are very noisy. Nobody sleeps. So on holiday I like to get away from them all and relax in peace. The Germans are well behaved and never late for meals. Hotels like them. They walk, they play tennis, they make themselves tired, and go to bed early."

"They still lay claim to the sun-beds," said Dotty indignantly, indicating the towels laid on all of them.

Roberto laughed. "No Dorothea," he said. "Don't make prejudices where there are none. The towels belong to the hotel. They are put out each morning by the pool attendant."

In the afternoon, on her way to her room for a siesta, Dotty spotted Helga at the reception desk with Luigi, her voice raised in querulous protest about something or other. Roberto was on easy terms with the staff and seemed to know all the gossip. She'd learned, during their conversation at the pool, that everyone loved the Professor and disliked Helga, who was jealous of the Professor's seniority. During the three years the conference had been held at the villa, she'd resorted to various underhand tricks to embarrass him. The first year, according to Roberto, the Professor had overslept and Helga, who as conference organiser should have ensured his presence, had left him to his slumbers so that he missed giving his keynote lecture on the final day. The staff had been so upset by this that the following year they'd asked one of the maids to wake him on conference days to make certain he was dressed and ready in time.

Dotty resolved to keep a beady eye on Helga.

———————————

CHAPTER NINE

It's extraordinary, thought Dotty, how quickly the foreign becomes familiar yet still retains its ability to surprise and delight. After only a few days at the villa, she was now uninhibitedly exchanging pleasantries with Gianni as she lay starkers in the mineral bath during her spa treatments. She'd already learned more about butterflies and moths than she'd ever imagined she'd want to know from amiable chats in the garden with the Professor.

She looked forward to her conversations each evening with Roberto across their dinner tables. The rest of the time they went their separate ways. Much as she enjoyed his company she was relishing, for the first time in her life the freedom to do as she pleased; to amble around the hotel's extensive grounds, thrash her way ungainly way across the swimming pool, duck behind a tree whenever the dreaded Helga clomped into view; to take guilt-free siestas.

She had surrendered to the gentle rhythm of life at the villa and was feeling completely at home. It was the empty, dusty house with its overgrown garden in Belmont Avenue that now seemed alien and far away. Although the Hotel Palladio was only the first stop on her tour, she was surprised at how far she'd already travelled in mind as well as body. Italy ravished her senses and seduced her eyes, encouraging her to stop and stare, to enjoy each day as it came.

Unusually for her, she'd felt no desire to rush off madly in all directions, and it was some days after her arrival that she set off one morning to explore Bellarosa and buy postcards and gifts for the family. Strolling through a warren of narrow streets, she smiled at the sight of laundry, like festive bunting, flapping gaily above her head; the clothes lines stretched between ingenious pulleys attached to window sills on either side of the streets. Shirts, tablecloths, dainty lace panties and Granny's baggy bloomers were pegged out in full view of those passing beneath. It wouldn't do to be on bad terms with your neighbours.

She was startled out of her reverie by a Vespa, ridden by what looked like a 5- year old wearing a safety helmet the size of a golf ball, which shot out of a side street and swerved past with the infuriated buzz of a giant wasp, forcing her to take a desperate leap out of its path. The peaceful routine at the Palladio has dulled my reflexes, she acknowledged, peeling herself off the wall as a couple of cats stretched themselves leisurely on a balcony and eyed her with suspicion.

She emerged from a dark alley into the sun-drenched square, the same one that had been slumbering under an enchanted spell when she'd first crossed it in the taxi. Today, the curtain had gone up on a brightly lit stage where the townsfolk were milling around like animated extras in a theatrical market-day scene. The dribbling Titan in the fountain, festooned with pigeons, was surrounded by stalls selling a cornucopia of fresh fruit and vegetables, household goods, cheeses and salami, shaded by gaily striped blue and white awnings.

It's magic, thought Dotty. Sheer magic.

Sitting at a pavement cafe, drinking a *cappucino*, she feasted her eyes on the passing scene, occasionally dipping into the guidebook she'd bought earlier that morning. In its literal English translation, it described lofty Bellarosa as "hanging over the valley in a very suggestive position." She had been made lazy by the seemingly effortless ease with which the hotel's staff spoke English. Her Italian language tapes languishing in a drawer since her arrival, she'd considered buying a phrasebook. Thumbing through one in the bookshop, she'd decided against it, unable to understand why they were so popular. It was pointless to ask "When do the trains leave for Milan?" if one was incapable of understanding the eruption of times, platforms and station changes which such a question would provoke.

Guidebook in hand she crossed the *piazza* to look inside the church. Half-hidden in the shadow of a buttress was a skinny nun in black habit and wimple, who, after a furtive glance around her, was taking a long and appreciative drag on a cigarette. At Dotty's approach she jumped like a clockwork toy before relieved recognition dawned.

"Blimey. You didn't half give me a fright," said the nun. "Thank God it's you."

"Nelly!" gasped Dotty. With her meringue of white hair hidden by the wimple, Nelly looked like a startled ferret.

"Sister Martha, if you don't mind," said Nelly. "And keep your voice down."

"What are you..." spluttered Dotty,

Glancing swiftly around her once more, Nelly dropped the cigarette end onto the cobbles and hitching up her skirts stubbed it out with her shoe. "I'm staying at one of the convents. Free in this outfit. I can save my bugs for another place."

"You're doing what?" exclaimed Dotty, aghast.

"It's not a bed of roses you know," said Nelly indignantly. "No mini-bar in the room and I have to get up at five to join in the prayers. Look funny if I didn't. Those stone floors aren't half playing hell with my knees."

"Don't they ask which convent you're from?" said Dotty.

"I said I'd just returned from Africa where I'd been working for years at a mission in the middle of nowhere," replied Nelly.

"But don't they check?" Dotty persisted.

"How?" asked Nelly. "Send a note in a cleft stick? Anyway, why would they bother? They don't expect nuns to tell whoppers."

A rotund cardinal, resplendent in scarlet surplice, black cape edged with scarlet piping and hat trimmed with scarlet ribbon and gold tassels, emerged from the church door, oozing self-satisfaction. He was accompanied by a deferential young priest in plain black cassock, carrying a briefcase, whom Dotty recognised as one of those on the plane coming over. The priest gave them a sweet smile. The Cardinal, in the midst of admonishing his acolyte, loftily acknowledged their presence with a condescending nod.

'No, no, no, Father," said the Cardinal, "He is not a Saint he is only a Blessed."

"See," said Nelly slyly to Dotty, once they were out of earshot. "Nobody's perfect."

After a quick stroll around the church, which to Dotty's Protestant eyes looked like a garishly decorated wedding cake, Nelly came to a halt beside an arched opening leading off a side aisle guarded by an elderly priest sitting at a small wooden table.

"Come on," she whispered to Dotty, "This you've got to see."

Dotty, noting a collection box on the table, fumbled for her purse but the priest shook his head.

"See," said Nelly, as they descended into the crypt, "nuns get a lot of respect over here."

"He could at least have charged *me* the entrance fee," said Dotty.

"Don't be daft," said Nelly. "It's criminal to have to pay in God's House."

As the pair reached the bottom step, Dotty paused in horror at what was displayed within the niches of stone arches supporting the church above.

"I bet you've never seen anything like this before," said Nelly, amused by Dotty's expression as her eyes skittered nervously over glass cases and frames of every shape and size containing holy relics: bones, coils of hair, and skulls of saints and martyrs, identified by yellowing tattered labels.

"I'd no idea saints were chopped up like this," said Dotty. "It's gruesome."

"Unfair, you mean," said Nelly. "Poverty stricken when they were alive; worth a fortune dead. You'd get a good price for these."

Dotty turned to her in astonishment. "People *buy* these?"

"General Franco kept St. Teresa of Avilla's arm in a box. Carried it everywhere with him," said Nelly.

"Everywhere?" asked Dotty.

"So they say. This is what comes of leading a saintly life," said Nelly, pointedly. "As soon as you're dead, everybody wants a bit. When St. Francis was taken to Assisi to be buried in the crypt, they locked the doors so nobody would know exactly where they'd put him; otherwise the body snatchers would have been there with their spades before you could say 'Robertson and Hare.' Most of the saints have been dug up and their bones shared out. Someone once worked out that if all the bits of St. Rita in reliquaries were genuine, she'd have had 35 fingers."

"So much for eternal rest," said Dotty.

"These bones have given me a thirst," said Nelly. "Fancy a drink and a bite to eat?"

Dotty gave her a warning look. "Only if you let me pay for us both," she said.

"I don't want your charity," said Nelly hotly. "I've got my pride."

"And I don't want to be put off my lunch again when you whip out your box of caterpillars," said Dotty.

"Oh well, in that case, love," said Nelly, "if it saves you embarrassment, thank you very much."

The pair seated themselves at a table in a simple, white-washed *trattoria* surrounded by the voluble chatter of fellow diners, who, from the evidence of grocery bags piled up around their feet, had come to Bellarosa for market day. Dotty, who had been biting on a breadstick when the waiter came over to take their order, choked on a crumb and went into a prolonged coughing fit as Nelly surprised her, yet again, by addressing him in fluent Italian.

"You...you..." Dotty gasped, as Nelly, clearly delighted at the effect she'd had, waited patiently for her to gulp down a glass of water. "You speak Italian."

"The mother of Arturo, my husband, was Italian. The family had a little milk bar in Soho in the fifties. I met him when I went to work there as a waitress..."

"...So, that was it," said Dotty a little later, having felt sufficiently relaxed now with Nelly to share confidences. "I sold the house and took off across Europe. The family wasn't too pleased."

"Raymond, that's my son, wasn't too pleased when I took off this time either," said Nelly. "Grumbled that there'd be no one to take him his cigs now he can't get out."

"Oh I am sorry," said Dotty, "is he an invalid?"

"In Wormwood Scrubs - for the umpteenth time," said Nelly, sounding disgusted.

She paused as the waiter came over with Dotty's order of liver with sage and her own ham hock. Dotty did her best to digest this latest revelation.

"I'm ashamed of him," said Nelly, once the waiter had left. "Always getting caught! *This* time, he'd nicked some lovely silver and when he got it home he saw one of the pieces was engraved 'With deepest love on our anniversary'. Sentimental is my Raymond. So next day he takes it back to number 64. Trouble was, he'd nicked it from number 62. Still, in fairness to him, them Georgian terrace houses all look alike. Number 64 had a big dog. Bit of a shock coming home to find your house broken into and a bleeding burglar on the rug who'd *brought* you a bonbon dish."

"And your husband?" Dotty asked, fearing the worst, "Where's he?"

Nelly took a swift look around her. "Not so loud," she hissed, "I'm supposed to be a nun. Died ten years ago. Came home one day with a suitcase full of cash. Said he'd buy me a fur coat. 'Not until you've laundered that lot, Arturo,' I said." She gave Dotty a baleful look. "Raymond overheard and thought he'd be helpful. The police were called to the laundrette before he'd got as far as spin dry. Two thousand quids' worth of sodden mush. It finished Arturo. He dropped dead of a heart attack a few days later."

Dotty marched furiously down the street, pursued by Nelly clutching a plastic bag. As Nelly grabbed her sleeve, trying to slow her down, Dotty shrugged her off roughly, attracting disapproving looks from passers by. Finally, she stopped and turned around.

"I told you I'd pay for you," said Dotty, her face contorted with anger.

"Couldn't help myself, could I," said Nelly. "It's daylight robbery the prices they were charging."

"That's no excuse," replied Dotty. "It's stealing. It was bad enough to get out of paying by dropping your caterpillar in the salad, but then to ask for a doggy bag for the ham bone. Really! Aren't they feeding you properly at the convent?"

"Don't be daft. It's not for me," said Nelly. "The Mother Superior's got a mongrel. Poor little thing lives on scraps. Thought I'd give him a treat."

Dotty felt hopelessly confused; unable to make sense of this jumbled morality. "Stay away from me, Nelly Broadbent," she warned, "or I'll...I'll..."

Nelly, unconcerned, gave her a broad grin. "You wouldn't thump a nun would you?" she asked. "Not in front of witnesses. You'd be lynched."

Dotty stomped up the drive to the hotel, berating herself for getting mixed up with Nelly Broadbent again. Her self-reproach vanished when she saw Professor Albrecht, emerging from behind an oleander bush, wearing a creased linen safari suit and panama hat. Clutching a butterfly net and specimen jar, he was quivering with excitement. His kindly face broke into a beatific smile as he caught sight of her.

"I have found it," he beamed, clutching her arm. "For many years I have been searching for a Red Underwing specimen to complete my collection.

How do you say it in English? 'the elusive butterfly'? Although, to be accurate, it is, in fact, a moth."

"Congratulations Professor! I'm so happy for you. But please promise me that you'll keep it in a safe place," said Dotty, thinking dark thoughts about Helga.

"I promise," said the Professor.

As Dotty followed his slow progress up the steps to the hotel's entrance, she sensed movement off to her left and caught a brief glimpse of a blonde head and the rear view of a pair of enormous khaki shorts. Helga quickly disappeared between the trees. From now on Helga, Dotty vowed, I'm going to watch you like a hawk.

Dotty lay on her bed, shutters closed against the diamond sharp intensity of the afternoon sun. She sighed, thinking about her latest encounter with Nelly. She didn't know what was right or wrong anymore. Nelly certainly hadn't had an easy life. She was beginning to realise just how fortunate she'd been, married to Ronald. Yes, he'd bored her with his 10 ton marrows, but he'd been kind, patient, given her complete security and two lovely daughters. She had much to be thankful for. And as for those morbid holy relics! Who'd want to end up as a saint? Thank goodness Ronald had been buried in an English churchyard: at least *he'd* still be there in one piece when she got back. Poor old Nelly. Two thousand pounds worth of mush. Even a half-wit would have known the money should have been dry cleaned.

Ravens like sinister portents emitting raucous croaks flitted across the sky, silhouetted against a giant silver moon. Dotty leant over a cauldron, slowly stirring its burping contents with an enormous wooden spoon, as the wood fire spat and crackled, throwing eerie shadows across her face. Ronald, flying astride a giant marrow, swooped down and, opening his arms, let fall a luminously colourful cascade of vegetables before vanishing into thin air. Dotty reached down, picked up a bunch of carrots and a couple of onions and chucked them into the cauldron.

Nelly, dressed in a nun's habit and witch's pointed hat, and riding a broomstick, hurtled out from behind a cloud and made a couple of rackety passes over Dotty's head, as she looked up at her with rueful amusement. Pointing the tip of her broomstick at the earth, Nelly came in to land at a staggeringly inappropriate speed. Hitting the ground with an almighty thud, the broomstick snapped, propelling her towards the fire where a spark ignited her habit and she combusted in a spectacular fiery display, leaving only a heap of scorched bones...

Dotty woke from her siesta dream in a complete

muck-sweat. Struggling to extricate herself from a tangle of twisted sheets, she fell back against the bed head, her heart thumping noisily in her ears, and turned for reassurance to Ronald, whose framed photograph was perched on the bedside cabinet.

"No more Nelly Broadbent, Ronald," she said. "I can get into enough trouble on my own."

CHAPTER TEN

Dotty dressed for dinner. She descended the staircase to the hall. Roberto, who'd been chatting to Luigi and the porter at the reception desk, walked across to join her at the bottom of the stairs.

"I was wondering," he murmured with feigned insouciance, "now we are better acquainted, if you would like to share my table for dinner from now on?"

Dotty's stomach did another of those little flips which Roberto's presence provoked. "That would be lovely," she said. "Thank you."

Smiling, Roberto offered her his arm. Dotty hesitated for a fraction of a second and then shyly slipped her arm through his. Luigi watched the couple as they made their stately progress across the hall to the dining terrace; nodding his head in approval as he saw Dotty look down at her arm through Roberto's then up at his handsome profile.

"*Molto romantico,*" he said. "It was a good idea to place them at tables side by side."

"You think it is love?" the porter queried.

Luigi shrugged. "Who knows. Whatever it is, it is making them happy."

"I was thinking," said Roberto when they'd settled themselves at his table, "that as this is your first time in Italy, you might wish to take a drive with me tomorrow - to Verona."

"Do you know," replied Dotty with endearing ingenuousness, "I've never been anywhere with a man other than my husband - apart from my son-in-law and he doesn't count - since the day we got married."

"Then Dorothea," said Roberto, "I think perhaps it is time you did."

Smiling happily, flattered by Roberto's invitation, Dotty glanced around the dining terrace and saw a grim-faced Madame Pompadour and a doleful Monsieur Pompadour looking in her direction. You don't have to be a fashion plate to attract the best-looking man in the hotel, she thought with unbecoming triumph.

"About tomorrow," said Roberto. "In Italy we think it is the men who should wear the trousers, so when we go to Verona…"

"You would like me to wear a dress," said Dotty.

"It would be a compliment to me," replied Roberto.

That will teach me to be smug, thought Dotty.

As Roberto studied the menu, she caught the eye of Professor Albrecht, who reminded her of that soppy English sheepdog in the paint commercial. Thrilled that he'd finally found his elusive moth, she gave him a big smile.

"If you like that man so much why you not sit at *his* table," said Roberto darkly, not looking up from the menu.

He must have eyes in the back of his head, thought Dotty. "But I wasn't..." she blustered, in shocked surprise.

"I would rather a woman was dead than see her excited by another man. You know what I mean?" said Roberto.

Dotty stared at him open mouthed. "But I…I wasn't."

"If a man does not feel the urge to murder a woman if she makes him jealous, then she cannot be a very special woman. You understand?"

"Well I..." spluttered Dotty, wondering how Ronald would have reacted if a rival had appeared and threatened their marriage. He'd have blamed himself, she thought fondly, for neglecting her; done his best to put things right and then, once harmony had been restored, disappeared once more into his greenhouse. She smiled.

"It is not a funny matter," said Roberto coldly, assuming she was laughing at him. "I knew a man once who kill his wife because she went with a much younger man. He was 70."

"The husband?" asked Dotty.

"The lover," Roberto replied, surprised by her question. "The husband was 85."

"The reason why I was smiling at the Professor," said Dotty, hoping to put an end to Roberto's murderous indignation, "was because I am so happy he's found it at last."

"Found what?" asked Roberto, his face alert with curiosity, his jealousy instantly forgotten.

Dotty told him about the Professor's capture of the Red Underwing moth and her sighting of Helga. "I just hope she doesn't find out before the conference," she said.

"She probably suspects already," replied Roberto, swivelling his eyes across to the Professor's table. "He looks so pleased with himself, I think maybe shortly he will explode."

"And by the way," said Dotty, unwilling to surrender her newly gained independence, "I am perfectly entitled to smile at anyone I wish."

Roberto, his face immobile, regarded her silently with his shrewd hazel eyes. Oh dear, that's torn it, she thought. Goodbye Verona.

"*Va bene* - very well," he said, finally, "but in Italy the women still allow their men to believe themselves strong and masterful. You understand what I am saying?"

"I'll think about it," said Dotty.

———————————————

CHAPTER ELEVEN

Roberto steered the car by remote control, being constitutionally incapable of talking without using both hands.

"What would happen if someone chopped your arms off?" asked Dotty, as they slammed down the *autostrada* to Verona.

"I'd be struck dumb" replied Roberto, amused by her question.

Dotty found driving in Italy an exhilarating experience. The Italians drove fast and competitively, the way she did; but with considerably more skill, as they didn't seem to hit so many things. Leaving Bellarosa, Roberto had calmly avoided an elderly mamma on a scooter who'd shot out of a side turning, her apron flapping in the wind, an over-laden basket of artichokes balanced precariously on her lap. At the bottom of the hill they'd overtaken a car being driven erratically; the driver deep in conversation with a youth on a bicycle who was travelling alongside, one hand outstretched, hanging on to the sill of the open car window. Geoffrey would have had a fit.

Dotty gazed in awe at a city of towers and Renaissance palaces built almost entirely of rosy pink marble. Even the pavements were marble, she noticed as they strolled past the Roman Arena where gladiators and wild animals had fought to the death two thousand years before. Crossing the spectacular Piazza dell Erbe, they entered the courtyard of Number 23 via Capello, which was crammed with excited, jostling tourists.

"And this," said Roberto with a flourish, pointing at a picturesque medieval house, "was the home of Giulietta. You know the most famous lovers in the world - Giulietta e Romeo?"

"Really?" replied Dotty, surprised. "You mean Romeo and Juliet."

"We Italians are more polite than the English," said Roberto. "We always put the lady first."

"But it's a play by Shakespeare," corrected Dotty

"We like to believe it was about two families who once lived in Verona - the Montecchi and Capuleti. The story was first written down by an Italian, Luigi da Porto. It was your Mr. Shakespeare who stole it," said Roberto.

"Shakespeare *didn't* steal it," retorted Dotty.

"Well I don't think signor da Porto gave it to him exactly," said Roberto, looking up at what was purported to be the balcony from which the real Giulietta had gazed down on Romeo.

"*Romeo, Romeo, wherefore art thou, Romeo..?*" quoted Dotty. "We studied the play at school. I remember thinking how sad it was to end the way it did."

"It is very romantic to die for love," said Roberto.

"Their families shouldn't have interfered," said Dotty, thinking of her own bossy mob.

"But the family always interferes," he replied, unperturbed. "Love dies but the family goes on for ever."

Later that morning, the pair ate lunch at a pavement cafe table as they listened to a group of student musicians seated on the steps of an adjacent Baroque palace, playing extracts from Gounod's "Romeo and Juliet". The music was suddenly drowned out by the joyous roar of a Ferrari which, with much unnecessary revving of the engine and squeal of tyres, the driver showily parked in front of the cafe. Aware of being the focus of admiring attention, an impossibly glamorous young couple emerged from the car and strolled off with their arms tightly wrapped around one another.

"Why are Italians so noisy?" Dotty asked.

"So we cannot hear ourselves think," said Roberto. "Thinking makes you old." He paused and refilled their wine glasses. "Tell me," he continued, curiosity replacing his usual good manners, "don't you miss your family?"

"They'll be there when I get back - eventually," said Dotty, clearly in no hurry to return.

"Who knows," he replied ominously. "Life is full of doubt."

"I didn't want to grow old thinking 'if only', said Dotty.

"But regretting can be nice," said Roberto. "Italians happily spend their lives regretting. Dreams are often better left as dreams. They can disappoint when you try to make them real."

Dotty pointed at the Ferrari. "Better to dream about a car like that than to drive it?"

"Ah, that is another point," he admitted, graciously acknowledging defeat. "Every Italian boy would like to have a Ferrari; to make a *bella figura* - cut a fine figure; the open road, a beautiful woman beside him."

"So, you *do* agree!" said Dotty.

Roberto shrugged. "*Si et no.* Mebbi it breaks down. Mebbi the woman sitting in the seat beside you is not Sophia Loren. If she had been, my wife would have killed me."

"It's never too late," said Dotty, encouragingly.

Roberto glanced down at his body. "Getting in might be OK but getting out would be a big problem now. And Sophia is not as young as she was either."

Dotty was silent for much of the journey back to Bellarosa, her thoughts occupied not only by the beauty of Verona but also by more mundane considerations: the seemingly effortless way in which the Italians appeared so stylish in contrast to the camera-festooned tourists: the men in open-necked shirts - some, horror of horrors, bare-chested in the heat; the women in inappropriately revealing low tops and shorts. Even those who courteously conformed to the city's dress code still lacked that indefinable something which made the Italians stand out from the foreign visitors.

She'd never bothered over much about her appearance; Ronald hadn't really noticed what she was wearing. On the odd occasions she'd sought his opinion - attending the wedding of a friend's daughter or Ladies Night at the Gardening Club, he'd been more concerned that her notoriously lax time-keeping would make them late rather than what she had chosen to wear. A fond "You look very nice, dear," followed by a quick glance at his watch had been his usual response.

Understandably, Dotty had packed for comfort when she set off on her travels and added only a couple of dresses for best. Unfortunately, best at the Hotel Palladio meant every evening. Although she had assumed she'd passed muster, otherwise Roberto wouldn't have been so attentive, in Verona he'd commented on the beautiful clothes artistically displayed in shop windows and suggested, none too subtly, that perhaps she should buy a new dress.

She hadn't expected freedom to be so complicated - or so expensive. By capitulating, would she be trying to become something she wasn't and had never been?

Should she continue to go her own sweet way if, now her circumstances had changed, another way might be sweeter? Certainly, the spa treatments and Roberto's interest had given her, belatedly, a new and disturbing awareness of her body.

As they drove into Bellarosa the shutters were being raised on shop windows as the town woke up after its *siesta* ,and Dotty came to a decision. She asked Roberto to drop her off in the piazza.

"*Guarda!* - Look," he said, winding down the car window and pointing across the square. "It is the mime troupe who will be appearing at the Palladio's theatre."

A small crowd had gathered at the bottom of the town hall steps where a number of loose-limbed young people dressed in black cat-suits, their faces painted white, were silently performing a mime to the accompaniment of a flute.

Dotty and Roberto watched as they mimed climbing an imaginary staircase, walking against a buffeting wind, and being chased back to shore by breakers as they paddled in a cold sea.

"*Meno male* - not bad," said Roberto, as Dotty got out of the car, "but I don't know if I would want to sit for a long time in a theatre watching this."

As Roberto drove off, Dotty saw Helga walk rapidly across the piazza and join a heavy set man seated at a pavement cafe table who appeared to have been waiting for her. Within seconds of her arrival, the couple were deep in conversation.

What's she up to, Dotty wondered, stepping back into the shadows beneath a shop awning as Helga glanced in her direction. What if she's plotting against the Professor? Dotty suddenly saw herself, like Miss Marple in an Agatha Christie crime novel, standing in the hotel's reception hall surrounded by admiring guests and staff as she triumphantly pointed an accusing finger at a cowering Helga. *"Why did she meet the infamous Mr. Lugosi at a cafe in Bellarosa? What was it she said to the man known to every police force in the world as The Butterfly Smuggler? The truth can now be told."*

Unfortunately, the reality didn't match her romantic fantasy; she was too far away to eavesdrop on their conversation. But if she moved closer, how could she keep Helga under surveillance without being recognised?

Stepping out of Roberto's air-conditioned car, she'd been surprised by how hot it still was in the late afternoon, the sun beating down remorselessly on her bare head. She glanced behind her through the window of the kind of old-fashioned general store selling an eclectic mixture of household goods including door mats, gardening tools, aprons and straw baskets that had sadly vanished from High Streets back home. I know what Miss Marple would have done, she thought, slipping inside.

She emerged from the shop a few minutes later carrying a small sunshade. Opening it, she raised it above her head then swiftly brought it down until it almost covered her face. With some difficulty, her vision restricted to passing ankles, she sidled up to the cafe and positioned herself in front of a tall shuttered house next door; within earshot, she hoped, of Helga and her companion.

Dotty stood rigidly immobile. Above her, a man in a white singlet, smoking a cheroot, was leaning on the sill of an upstairs window of the house, watching the mime troupe. Without checking the street below, he carelessly flicked the lighted stub out of the window. In one of those perverse tricks of fate whereby a bull's eye is inadvertently scored, it was stopped in its downward spiral by the sunshade.

A fat lot of good this subterfuge has done me, Dotty berated herself. She'd failed to consider the obvious: that Helga would be speaking in her native German or possibly in Italian. The provincial Miss Marple hadn't had this problem - *her* murder suspects tended to be country house types with cut-glass English accents.

Wondering how best to make a hasty exit without alerting Helga, she was disconcerted to see that the truncated bodies of passers-by were no longer passing but coming to a sudden halt in front of her. Assuming

Dotty was an adjunct to the mime troupe's performance or, if not, a spectacle too ripe in possibility to cut short just yet, no one bothered to warn her that the brolly was beginning to smoulder. Oh this is hopeless, she thought, how do spies make themselves invisible? And what's that acrid smell?

Alerted by the rising smoke, the man at the window, looking down in alarm, swiftly removed a bunch of lilies from a vase on the window sill and, leaning out, poured the contents of the vase onto the brolly beneath him.

Dotty jumped visibly at the impact, stunned by the sight of water cascading down around her. Peering out from under her brolly at a cloudless sky as onlookers broke into spontaneous applause, she rose magnificently to the occasion. She bowed.

"*Complimenti!*" "*Brava!*" "*Bellissima!*" chorused members of the mime troupe who had run across the square to join her.

"Thank you," replied Dotty, graciously accepting their plaudits. The world's gone mad, she thought, and my cover's been blown. Helga was staring at her with an expression of disapproval and, she had to admit, suspicion.

"English?" asked the young man.

"Yes," said Dotty.

"From one *artiste* to another signora, our compliments," he said. "I am Alessandro, call me

Sandro, and this is Fiametta and this is Pietro."

"What artistry! What timing! What splendid economy of movement," said Pietro, shaking his head in admiration.

"Thank you," replied Dotty. There was no going back now.

"You will be performing again tomorrow?" asked Fiametta, eagerly.

"Oh no," said Dotty, "I've retired."

"Ah," said Sandro, "that was just for old times sake eh? With your friend upstairs?" He glanced up at the now empty window.

Dotty nodded.

"We are performing at the Hotel Palladio tomorrow evening. We go to rehearse now. Will you come? We would value your experience."

"Oh, I've forgotten most of what I knew," Dotty replied modestly, folding her sunshade, "but I'm staying at the Palladio and I'd love to come with you."

Walking up the drive to the hotel accompanied by Sandro, Fiametta and Pietro, mulling over her disastrous attempt to spy on Helga, Dotty remembered she'd forgotten to buy a dress. Oh what does it matter, she thought. Do as the Italians appear to do. Enjoy each moment as it comes. If she hadn't made such a fool of herself in Bellarosa for reasons which she was still unable to fathom, she wouldn't have met these delightful young people who were playfully weaving a figure of eight around her, chirruping happily like bright-eyed eager sparrows, as they headed in the direction of the theatre.

Although there were nine members in the troupe, Sandro explained, the others had stayed behind to make everything ready for the rehearsal. He and his two companions had gone into Bellarosa hoping that their appearance in the *piazza* would boost the, as yet, depressingly poor ticket sales for their production the following evening. The experimental work they would be performing at the theatre had been conceived by Sandro who, rather than taking part, would be directing it.

The Teatro Palladio was a faded jewel casket of a miniature theatre, with red velvety plush seats below and tiers of intimate boxes above decorated with gilded friezes of yet more cheekily grinning cherubs. Heavy red curtains were looped back on either side of the stage and elfin-like lanterns illuminated the tiny orchestra pit.

"For the performance," said Sandro, "I have hired a little orchestra to accompany us, but it is a big expense so for the rehearsals we use recorded music."

Music was not how Dotty would have described the tuneless discordant noises which assailed her ears, rendered even more excruciating by the accompanying strangled wailings of the cast, who now appeared on stage wearing extraordinary multi-coloured padded costumes like psychedelic Michelin-men. For the next half-hour, watched by a bewildered Dotty, they conjoined and separated in a series of sinuous movements interspersed with sudden, frozen, contorted postures.

Sandro flapped around like one of Professor Albrecht's butterflies as he directed the cast; alighting briefly on the edge of a seat, flitting nervously up the aisle, vanishing from the auditorium before suddenly reappearing on stage as if he'd been teleported, swooping down on the performers to arrange or rearrange their poses. Dotty, at a complete loss to understand what was going on, found it increasingly difficult not to let her incomprehension show as Sandro glanced from time to time in her direction.

The cast took a ten-minute break and, to Dotty's immense relief, the caterwauling ceased. Sandro flopped down into the seat beside her, limply exhausted by his creative efforts.

"In Zen Buddhism, it is said that when you climb a mountain it is the mountain as much as your own legs that lifts you upwards. Interesting, eh? "

"Very," said Dotty, dissimulating frantically.

"In Bellarosa, we were miming actions which people could recognise," he explained earnestly, "but this is an experimental piece to make the audience see familiar things in a different way. The artist Miro described his drawings as 'taking a line for a walk'. We are trying with our bodies to write sentences in space. The flowing movements are the words, the pauses are the punctuation - commas, full stops, question marks. You understand?"

"Sort of poetry in motion?" asked Dotty, making an inspired guess.

Sandro looked at her in astonishment and clapped his hands. "*Brava!*" he said. "*Perfetto.*"

Sometimes, thought Dotty, I don't know how I do it.

"So, what do you think?" he asked.

For someone whose theatre-going had been confined to drawing room comedies and the occasional musical, to which she could sing along, she didn't know what to think. "I'm sure it will be a huge success," she replied with as much sincerity as she could muster, not wishing to hurt Sandro's feelings.

"I am hoping so," he said, sighing dramatically. "My friend, he gives me the money to pay for the theatre. He has paid for theatres before. Always I fail. He says this is my last chance. The brute."

Dotty squeezed his hand in sympathy, silently willing him to succeed. This is how youth should be, she thought, doing crazy incomprehensible things; learning together; having fun, and, she had to admit, remembering her own daughters' teenage years, being supported by indulgent adults. Sandro, she'd learned, was a professional ballet dancer who'd been with a company that had recently disbanded. Unable to find another position, he'd invited the others, all ballet students on holiday, to join him for a summer season of mime.

The troupe was staying on a campsite near Bellarosa but the hotel had generously provided a picnic supper, which Fiametta was unpacking on the grass. Dotty was relieved as well as pleased to accept their invitation to share it with them. Roberto was spending the evening at the home of friends in Padova and his absence had presented her with a dilemma. Should she return to what had been her table or sit at Roberto's as she had the previous evening? Wherever she'd sat she'd have felt uncomfortable under the watchful gaze of Madame Pompadour, who'd have reached her own conclusions as to why she was alone. What's happening, she wondered, I've never cared before about what other people think of me.

Joining the others in a circle on the grass, happily tucking in to salami and prosciutto, cold stuffed aubergines, juicy black olives, fruit, cheese and crusty bread, Dotty told her appreciative audience about Ronald's garden and horticultural triumphs.

"We Italians think we have the best food in the world," said Sandro, "but when I was in the ballet company we went to England and I fell in love with Lincolnshire pork sausages. After a performance I would always eat - what do you call them - bangers? When I am under pressure, like now, I long for them. Interesting no?"

"Very," said Dotty.

"You didn't perhaps bring some with you?" he asked with naive optimism.

"It wasn't something that crossed my mind," said Dotty. "I am sorry." There was something else she regretted: not being truthful about what had happened in Bellarosa. She told them about Professor Albrecht and Helga and why she had been standing like a pillar of salt by the cafe. They, in turn, cleared up the mystery of the sudden downpour.

"I'm sorry I gave the impression I was performing," she said

"We knew you were pretending," said Pietro.

"But you did it so well," said Fiametta.

The light was fading when Dotty rose unsteadily to her feet, having consumed far too much wine. "Thank you all very much," she said, looking down fondly on the upturned faces, "I've had a lovely time."

Sandro jumped up and kissed her on both cheeks. "We will see you again tomorrow evening. You must stay for the party afterwards."

"I shall look forward to it," said Dotty, wondering how she could go through that a second time. "*Buona notte."*

As the troupe cleared away the picnic, Sandro turned to Pietro: "*Il parcoscenico e troppo scivolosa. Per favore, mettete un' litro di aqua e limone prima di domani sera. Questa volta, non devo falire,*" he said - The stage is still too slippery. Please put a litre of lemon juice on it before tomorrow night. This time I must not fail.

The doors to the balcony were open framing a crescent moon as delicate as a child's fingernail; the star of Venus gleaming gold. As Dotty emerged from the bathroom after cleaning her teeth, the silence was filled by the soaring voice of an operatic tenor singing *Nessun Dorma*.

Roberto, holding a red rose, was standing beneath her window with a torch pushed down inside the belt of his trousers, the beam directed at his feet providing a mini spotlight. He was miming to the Pavarotti recording. His lip movements were convincingly in synch until he suddenly doubled over in a coughing fit while the recording continued. Regaining control with admirable aplomb, he resumed his mimetic aria until, bracing himself as the music built to its climax, his mouth opened and closed ever more slowly as the recording ground to a *basso profundo* halt.

He opened his jacket to reveal a small cassette machine hanging around his neck.

"My battery has died!" he called. "I am so sorry"; whereupon they both burst out laughing.

He tossed the rose up to Dotty, who clutched wildly at thin air as the flower fell back at his feet. Shaking his head in mock sorrow he tried again. This time, leaning perilously over the balcony rail, she caught it but in her clumsy eagerness dislodged a pot of geraniums suspended from the rail. With a muttered oath, Roberto leapt back as it shattered to smithereens at his feet.

"*Buona notte, Giulietta,*" he called up to her, "I think you will make sure I die for you." With a wave of his hand, he was gone.

Dotty remained on the balcony, her nose buried in the rose. All those romantic novels she'd read over the years in which women pined, men desperately fought off rivals and love triumphed, or, like Romeo and Juliet, the lovesick died in despair, she had reluctantly dismissed as fiction. But since meeting Roberto she'd been getting a funny, tingling feeling in her stomach as if she was sickening for a gastric attack.

Was she just another pitiful woman of a certain age who was following in the footsteps of all those other English romantics in the grip of an Italian fantasy? Was this just a game to be enjoyed light-heartedly or one that she didn't know how to play? Nothing in her life had prepared her for this.

She crossed to the bathroom, filled a tumbler with water and returned to her bedroom. Self-consciously aware of Ronald's eyes on her, she dropped the rose into the glass and placed it on the other bedside cabinet distancing it from Ronald.

About to pull back the covers, she was shocked to see Roberto in her bed. His naked bronzed torso partly wrapped toga-like in the white sheet, a wreath of laurel leaves crowning his silver hair, he was seductively offering her a grape from a lusciously ripe bunch on his lap. With a startled cry, Dotty slammed Ronald's photograph down on the bedside table, her heart pounding. At your age, she admonished herself. You should be ashamed of such fantasies!

CHAPTER TWELVE

Ronald was spending an increasing amount of his time flat on his face in the top drawer of the bedside cabinet. Dotty, wrestling with her feelings for Roberto and fearing Ronald could read her thoughts, was no longer able to look him in the eye.

You're not being disloyal, she told herself. You're a widow. Life must go on. You're free to make a fool of yourself. Do it now before you lose your resolve. What was it she'd said to Roberto in Verona? "I don't want to grow old thinking 'if only'."

She went to consult the hotel's Mr. Fix-it.

"Luigi," said Dotty. "Can you keep a secret?"

"Of course I can, signora Lucas," he assured her solemnly.

"I'd like you to hire a Ferrari for me."

Dealing with guests over the years Luigi had become professionally adept at never showing his irritation at their often demanding requirements or petty complaints. But this time it was difficult to hide his delighted astonishment.

"*Mi dispiace* - I am sorry, *signora,* but I cannot do that," he said, lamenting his inability to grant her wish *and* provide them all with an unforgettable spectacle.

"But I thought you could arrange anything," said Dotty, looking crest-fallen. "It's signor Carducci's birthday in a couple of days. I wanted to give him a nice surprise."

To say nothing of a heart attack, thought Luigi. Really, the English never failed to astonish him; they were the most unpredictable of all the nationalities which stayed at the hotel. "It is a beautiful idea," he said. "A romantic idea - but impossible. You cannot hire Ferraris in Italy. No company would provide insurance. They are too tempting for thieves."

"That's typical of the world today," said Dotty in a huff, "honest people being denied fun because of a few crooks."

Luigi tried his best to be helpful. "Perhaps *you* could steal one. Maybe you could find someone who has stolen one who will lend it to you."

The trouble with Italians, thought Dotty, was that you were never sure when they were joking. "Promise you won't say anything to anybody about this," she pleaded.

"I promise," said Luigi. Much as he relished the thought of sharing the secret with other members of the hotel staff, it would be worth waiting to see what she would do next. She didn't seem the type who'd take no for an answer.

Dotty stomped off to her room and telephoned Painless Travel.

"Mrs Lucas," Nigel greeted her nervously, "where are you?"

"Still at the Hotel Palladio."

"Oh good," he said, "I'm very relieved to hear it."

"Listen Nigel," said Dotty. "You know Burtons the butchers in the precinct?"

"Er... yes," he replied with understandable caution.

"I need ten pounds of Lincolnshire pork sausages for a party this evening. You'll have to fax them to me."

"Pardon?" said Nigel, "I can't do that."

"Nigel," said Dotty, annoyed, "I do wish you'd stop being difficult."

"I am not being difficult," he protested. "You can't fax sausages."

Give me patience, thought Dotty. First it was Luigi and now Nigel. "As I understand it," she said, "what you put in at your end comes out at my end. Yes or no?"

"In a manner of speaking," said Nigel.

"Well then," said Dotty, "What's your problem?"

"BUT...IT...WON'T...DO...FOOD!".

Dotty thought it wise to remain silent and give him a moment to calm down. In truth, she only had the vaguest idea about how a fax machine worked so he might be right. "There's one other thing," she said, finally. "I want you to hire a Ferrari for me."

"You want me to do WHAT?" squealed Nigel.

"You heard," said Dotty.

"Oh no, no, no, Mrs. Lucas," he moaned. "It's too

dangerous. Ferraris aren't cars, they're jet-propelled rockets."

"It's impossible to hire one over here," said Dotty with unbecoming slyness. "I thought it would be one in the eye for the Italians if you succeeded where they'd failed -Your patriotic duty. Flying the flag and all that. But if you *can't* do it."

"Of course I *could* do it," he replied foolishly. "Nigel can do anything. But I won't. I've never lost a client yet."

"Oh it's not for me," said Dotty. "It's for an *Italian* to drive. Even more reason to show what *we* can do."

"I won't. I won't. I won't," said Nigel.

"Oh yes you will," said Dotty. "I'm relying on you."

Why does everything have to be so complicated, she thought, frustrated by the morning's events and the necessity of depending upon others to realise her wishes. All I wanted was to give Sandro and Roberto a treat. At least she could do something herself about the third item on her list. Determined not to be distracted yet again, she set off for Bellarosa to buy a new dress to wear for the mime troupe's performance that evening.

The first boutique she tried had nothing she liked in her size. Directed to another shop by the kindly assistant, she lost her way in the shadowy labyrinth of side streets. Trying to get her bearings from a brief, tantalising glimpse of the piazza in the distance, she took what she hoped would be a short cut down a narrow passage. She emerged in a tranquil cloistered garden just as a black-clad figure, skirts hitched high, hurtled from behind a pillar and collided forcefully with her, almost knocking her off her feet as something clattered to the ground.

"I might have known I'd bump into *you* again!" gasped Dotty.

"Phew! You gave me a right turn," said Nelly, taking great gulps of air as she frantically scanned the paving for whatever it was she'd dropped in the collision.

But Dotty saw it first. Stooping to pick up the bone, she sighed, "You didn't tell me the truth, did you?"

"What?" said Nelly, making a sudden lunge at Dotty.

Dotty held the bone at arm's length above her head as little Nelly, making bathetic attempts to snatch it from her, leapt up and down as if trying to score at netball.

"It wasn't for the dog was it?" said Dotty, visibly upset. Perhaps Nelly had finally run out of restaurants to cheat in Bellarosa.

"Just give it to me for heaven's sake," hissed Nelly as the mongrel appeared, sniffing around the cloisters.

Seeing the bone, the dog did what a dog knows

how to do best. It sat on its haunches very politely and fixed Dotty with pleading, patient eyes.

"Pride is all very well, you know," said Dotty patronisingly, "but I can't have you going hungry like this."

She threw the bone to the mongrel which caught it expertly and scampered off through the cloisters. Nelly, with an agonised yelp, set off in pursuit. Dotty's arm shot out and, clutching the folds of her wimple, dragged her backwards.

"Forget about it," she said, as Nelly twisted around in a fury desperately trying to break free. "I'll buy you lunch."

"You're a proper little Goody Two Shoes, aren't you," spat Nelly. "Why can't you mind your own soddin' business."

"It's only a bone," said Dotty, shocked by her vehemence.

"It happens to be St. Anthony's knuckle," corrected Nelly.

"What?" said Dotty loosening her grip on Nelly.

Nelly pulled her back into the shadows of the cloisters.

"It was in a glass case in the Mother Superior's room. Five hundred quid I could have got for that."

"You stole it?"

"I replaced it," said Nelly self righteously.

"With what?" asked Dotty. But she already knew

the answer. Oh no! Not with the ham bone."

"St. Anthony's often seen in paintings surrounded by piglets," said Nelly.

Dotty bit her lip, trying to suppress a smile. "Oh Nelly, how could you!"

"I'm getting out of here," said Nelly, "If someone notices they might start checking my religious credentials. And gawd knows where the dog will bury St. Anthony."

"But what about your luggage?" asked Dotty. "You can't leave without..."

"Do you think I'm stupid!" retorted Nelly. "I left my suitcase in a locker at the airport. What would a nun be doing with anti-wrinkle cream and frilly undies?"

Before they could make their getaway, the mongrel reappeared with the bone still clamped between its jaws. Nelly pounced upon the bone but the dog, happy to prolong the game, did a swift about turn and trotted in through the open door of a room leading off the cloisters.

"That's torn it. I'm off." said Nelly, "That's the Mother Superior's room."

"I'm staying," said Dotty recklessly. "This is too good to miss. There must be a window somewhere."

"Follow me," said Nelly, curiosity having swiftly replaced her fear.

Looking carefully to left and right, she skirted the

cloisters with Dotty close behind and took an overgrown path leading to the back of the convent. Half way down she pointed at a small barred window open at the top. Flattening herself against the wall, Dotty peered in cautiously as Nelly crouched beside her, peeking in over the sill.

The whitewashed room was sparsely furnished with a simple wooden table, a couple of chairs and beneath a painting of the Madonna and Child a low cabinet on which stood the reliquary case containing the ham bone; it's hinged glass door slightly ajar. St. Anthony's knuckle was lying on the tiled floor.

"It gets worse," whispered Nelly "I thought I'd closed the case. Time to scarper." As she scrambled to her feet, Dotty pushed her down again.

The pair watched as the mongrel, sniffing the air, pattered over to the reliquary and puts its paws up on the cabinet in an attempt to reach the ham bone. Nudging the front of the case with its nose, it inadvertently pushed the door closed just as a couple of nuns entered the room.

"Oh blimey," said Nelly. "The taller one's the Mother Superior"

"Romolo!" gasped the Mother Superior, staring in horror at St. Anthony's knuckle on the floor and the dog scrabbling at the glass case. Frowning, she said something sharply to the dog.

Dotty nudged Nelly. "What did she say?" she

whispered.

Nelly put her finger to her lips. "I'll tell you later," she mouthed.

Frustrated as she was at not being able to understand what was being said, Dotty nevertheless had little difficulty in following the scene being played out before her. Here we go again, she thought. More mime.

Picking up St. Anthony's knuckle, the Mother Superior walked over to the reliquary case and stared in bewilderment at its contents. Reverently placing St. Anthony on the table, she unlatched the glass door and studied the ham bone in silence as the nun, watching her closely, crossed herself. Smiling beatifically, the Mother Superior beckoned the nun to join her and pointed at the ham bone. Although Dotty couldn't understand a word that was said, their obvious delight was blatantly apparent. After carefully closing the door of the reliquary case and ensuring the latch was secure, the Mother Superior bustled out of the room taking St. Anthony's knuckle with her; the nun and the mongrel following merrily in her wake.

Dotty and Nelly didn't stop running until they were safely back in the side streets of Bellarosa.

"Come on," said Dotty impatiently after they'd paused to catch their breath, "Tell me what they said and make sure it's the truth."

"Don't worry," Nelly assured her, trembling with excitement. "It's better than anything I could make up. The Mother Superior told Romolo he'd committed a terrible sin stealing St. Anthony's knuckle but when she saw the ham bone which still had some bits of meat on it, she thought the *dog* must have swopped them around and made his own special offering to God."

"Offering?" repeated Dotty, looking puzzled.

"If *you* were a dog," said Nelly, "which bone would be more precious to you: - the Saint's musty old knuckle or a nice meaty ham bone? Anyway," she continued, "that's how the Mother Superior interpreted it. She thinks it's a miracle and she's shot off to spread the glad tidings."

"I don't know how you keep getting away with it," said Dotty, "you have the luck of the devil."

"Oh ye of little faith," retorted Nelly piously. "God loves sinners. He's used me to give the Vatican a wake-up call. Romolo could be the first animal in history to be made a Blessed."

"You seem to have conveniently forgotten that *I* was the one who gave the saint's bone to the dog," corrected Dotty, "*You* were going to steal it."

"That's true," agreed Nelly. "I must remember to give you some of the credit when I make my next Confession."

"Don't you dare bring my name into it," said Dotty,

regretting her moment of vanity.

"Please yourself," said Nelly.

"Come to think of it," said Dotty, "you're faced with something of a moral dilemma. If you do tell the truth about what happened it'll be goodbye to a Blessed Romolo."

Nelly grinned. "Wrong again Dorothy," she said, "I'm protected by the secrets of the confessional box. It's the *priest* who'll have to wrestle with his conscience."

CHAPTER THIRTEEN

Relieved that she'd emerged unscathed from her foolhardy impulse to remain longer than was wise at the convent, Dotty made her excuses and left Bellarosa. One day, she promised herself, she'd buy a new dress.

Back at the hotel, she telephoned Nigel in response to a message he'd left with reception and ate a quick lunch at the salad bar by the pool. Seeing Professor Albrecht reading under the trees she was reminded, guiltily, that she hadn't given Helga another thought since leaving Bellarosa the previous day. After he'd reassured her that the precious specimen was still in his possession, she returned to her room for a much needed siesta. It was all very well being part of life's rich tapestry but her adventures with Nelly invariably left her feeling distinctly frayed around the edges.

In the early evening she strolled over to the theatre to wish Sandro and the cast success. The theatre was unlocked, but on entering she found the place deserted. The troupe must be resting before the evening's performance. Dotty had never been alone in an empty theatre before, and was disconcerted by its melancholy atmosphere; as if the building was waiting for the actors, audience, lights and music to reaffirm its reason for existing.

She breathed in its unique aroma of greasepaint, the acrid odour of size for stiffening scenery and an all-pervading fustiness, and stepped tentatively, for the first time, onto a stage. Surprised by how steeply it sloped down to the footlights, she wondered why it had never occurred to her before that it had to be like that, otherwise much of the action would not have been visible to an audience.

Gazing out across the auditorium she was unable to resist the temptation of reciting the only poem she could remember in its entirety:

> *'Is there anybody there?' said the Traveller*
> *Knocking on the moonlit door;*
> *As his horse in the silence champed the grasses*
> *Of the forest's ferny floor;*
> *And a...................... '*

Dotty tailed off, overcome by a creepy sensation that as soon as the words left her mouth they were being swallowed up greedily by the huge gaping mouth of the auditorium, which waited hungrily to be fed. Not a good choice, she scolded herself; too spooky.

Refusing to be intimidated she yelled defiantly:

> *"The boy stood on the burning deck*
> *His feet were full of blisters.*
> *He tore his trousers down the back*
> *And had to wear his sister's. "*

This time the ghosts must have found her choice

indigestible, for it seemed to Dotty that the words were flung back at her contemptuously from the echoing void.

Feeling suddenly vulnerable and exposed, she turned on her heels to leave the stage, jumping in fright as the soles of her plimsolls squeaked in protest.

Halting in mid-flight, she bent down and ran her fingers across the boards. Yuk. The stage was sticky. Young people, she thought with fond indulgence. The troupe must have been so busy rehearsing, feet tramping across the stage, that they'd either forgotten or more likely couldn't be bothered to clean it. Searching around backstage she unearthed a bucket and mop propped beside a sink half hidden by a rack of costumes.

Seated beside Roberto in one of the boxes waiting for the performance to begin, Dotty peered over the balcony. She was disappointed to see that the stalls were only half full.

In a courteous gesture to Sandro and no doubt in the hope of increasing ticket sales, dinner had been served an hour early to give the waiters and kitchen staff the opportunity to attend if they wished. She was gratified to see that, like the hotel guests, they'd all turned up to support the troupe. Other than a sprinkling of townspeople she thought she recognised from Bellarosa, the strangers in the audience she swiftly and probably not inaccurately, identified from their appearance as students, bohemians or, in the case of an older, cosmopolitan contingent of men with beards or bow-ties accompanied by a few self-consciously chic young women, as po-faced critics and hangers-on.

Sandro, greeting the latter in turn, was looking intensely nervous, flouncing around, hopping from foot to foot.

The murmurings in the audience ceased as the conductor raised his baton and the orchestra launched into an ear-aching atonal overture with such force that it sounded as if they were trying to beat it into submission. When its anti-climax petered out around the auditorium and the heavy curtains parted with an audible swish, Dotty was pleased with what she saw.

"The stage was all sticky when I called in this afternoon," she whispered to Roberto, wrinkling up her nose, "so I gave it a really good wash and polish."

Roberto turned his head very slowly and stared at her with wide, unblinking eyes, his desire to save Dotty by leaping to his feet and alerting Sandro wrestling with his longing to witness the potentially devastating consequences of her innocent meddling.

But it was already too late. Leaning forward in his seat, he gripped the edge of the box, his body tense with anticipation as Pietro, howling like a coyote in its death throes to the orchestra's plonking accompaniment, strode onto the stage.

With a painful backward jerk as if he'd been rammed from behind, his feet shot out from under him and, involuntarily miming tobogganing on a tin tray, he was propelled with considerably velocity downstage and into the orchestra pit where, to his own and the audience's audible astonishment, he landed gracefully on his feet between two of the musicians.

Dotty gasped as if she'd been punched in the stomach and clutched the arms of her chair, fighting to quell her mounting terror that this was no accident. Although it was to the musicians' considerable credit that they didn't miss a beat as Pietro unexpectedly dropped in on them, their professionalism may well have contributed to what happened next, for the rest of the troupe, obeying their familiar musical cue, almost immediately followed Pietro onto the stage in blissful ignorance of what was about to befall them. Lined up shoulder to shoulder behind the backcloth, they marched forward with military precision as it rose and collapsed *en masse* as if shot by a firing squad.

Sliding uncontrollably, cannoning into each other's prostrate bodies, they came to rest in a tangled heap perilously close to the edge of the stage, as the musicians, in an act of collective self-preservation flattened themselves against the sides of the orchestra pit in a cacophony of jangling notes.

Dotty, stifling her compulsion to giggle, was hit by a blood-draining wave of nausea as her worst fears were confirmed. Sandro, who'd spent the entire day strung up on a high wire of pre-performance tension, passed out.

Whether it was the spectators' palpable air of hushed expectation or their own professional pride which impelled them to continue, no one will ever know; but the cast rose magnificently to the unexpected challenge. To the wonderment of the audience, they launched themselves into a breath-taking display of acrobatic mimes which proved conclusively that even the most supple, trained young bodies were no match for a slippery slope.

To the accompaniment of cheers they rose, they fell, they rose again; flapping their arms like pioneer aviators, scything the air like windmills, spinning like tops or insensible dervishes, they tried with varying degrees of success to maintain their balance while the orchestra played on and the audience collapsed into happy hysteria.

Struggling back to consciousness after his fainting fit, Sandro heard through the rush of blood hammering in his ears the muted sound of what he assumed to be mocking laughter. About to sink once more into welcome oblivion, his eye was caught by a large goatee-bearded man, his face wet with tears, who roared *"Fantastico! Stupendo!"* Before an astonished Sandro could react, a critic further along the row called *"Bravo maestro!"* and shook his head in almost reverential approval. Rapidly regaining his wits, Sandro responded like the true artiste he was with an overly modest shrug of his shoulders.

Dotty, radiant with relief, tears of laughter glistening on her cheeks, glanced at Roberto. Sensing her eyes on him, he turned to her briefly and, reaching out, took her hand in his, squeezing it in sympathetic understanding.

Pietro, who'd been given a kindly leg-up by the flautist resting before his next cue, had wriggled back over the edge of the stage. Bent double with the effort he was inching his way laboriously up the incline. Every step he took and tried to follow with the other foot, the one with which he'd taken the first step slid downstage again followed by the other one - in unconscious homage to Marcel Marceau's *Marche en place* - marching on the spot - before he fell flat on his face.

He'd just risen to his feet once again, arms flailing in an heroic attempt to remain upright, when Fiametta, transported downstage as if running on silken rails, shunted him back onto his knees with her sprawled body on top. Arms wrapped around one another, they crawled crablike across the stage, grimly determined to reach the safety of one of the curtains. Urged on by the audience Pietro lunged repeatedly at the curtain, his fingers tantalisingly close. With one final heave of his body he stretched out his arm and grasped the edge of the curtain as Fiametta clung to his legs. .

Someone grabbed Fiametta's arm and hung on. Another performer clutched the grabber, another grabbed the clutcher and so on, until they were all hanging on to each other, those on the end slipping downstage, their legs dangling over the edge.

The curtain track, straining to support the ever-increasing weight, finally gave way. With a protesting shriek of tearing fabric accompanied by a quick-witted musician's reverberating roll on the drums, the heavy curtain came down in a cloud of ancient dust, burying the troupe beneath it in a glorious finale.

Wriggling free of its suffocating folds, the cast sensibly chose to leave the stage by sliding into the orchestra pit and scrambling up the other side into the front stalls.

Joined by the visibly wilting conductor and musicians, they reassembled in a ragged exhausted line as the audience leapt to its feet with roars of appreciation.

Sandro remained seated while his gallant troupe triumphantly acknowledged the applause during numerous curtain-less curtain calls. n he could milk the insistent cries of "*Maestro! Maestro!"* no longer, he rose with studied reluctance and gave a master class in humility: bowing deeply before redirecting the applause with a theatrical sweep of his arm to the true stars of the night's revels.

Those who'd been privileged to share the occasion would struggle unsuccessfully in the years to come to recapture that sadly rare sense of joyous abandonment which the evening had bestowed upon them. If a few harboured a faint suspicion that what they'd witnessed had arisen by accident rather than design, they didn't care.

Weak from laughter, the couple who did know the truth stood in their box and clapped until their arms ached and their palms stung. About to leave the box and join the backstage party, Roberto stopped Dotty with a restraining arm, knowing from the determined look on her face what she was planning to do.

"Wait," he said. "Listen to me. First rule of life: Never, never explain."

"But…"

"If the evening had been a disaster, you would have confessed?"

"Of course," said Dotty "It would have been my fault."

"So," Roberto continued, "You think that if the

young people were lying in hospital beds with broken arms and heads, your confession would have made them feel better? Or just made your conscience feel better?"

"Well I..."

"But it was a big success because the young people were fantastic and made it a success. You want to take some of that praise for yourself?"

"Of course not, but..." stuttered Dotty.

"You are not in England now," said Roberto gently, "We have different, more ancient ways of doing things. You understand?"

"I think so," said Dotty, "but..."

"No buts," warned Roberto, squeezing her arm. "Now let's go and enjoy ourselves."

And they did enjoy themselves. They looked on in delight as Sandro and his cast, grinning like Cheshire Cats, submitted to a barrage of kisses and compliments. When, at last, Dotty was able to push her way through the crowd to congratulate them, she felt a momentary twinge of unease. It was difficult to suppress the moral duty instilled in childhood to own up to one's transgressions. It might have been easier if she'd known that her parents, called upon with alarming regularity to sort out yet another mess her impulsiveness had caused, had often wished she'd kept the truth to herself. In the event, she accepted - at least for now - the wisdom of Roberto's advice.

CHAPTER FOURTEEN

To ensure guests were not late for their tightly scheduled treatments, the receptionist in the spa annexe called their rooms 15 minutes before the appointed time. This morning, however, Luigi was on the line when Dotty answered her telephone.

"We are asking guests if they would be kind enough to go without their treatments today so that we can give *signor* Alessandro's troupe massage and physiotherapy. I am sure you will understand," said Luigi.

"Of course," said Dotty, her continuing elation at the previous night's events now shattered by embarrassed concern as the line went dead. Had she detected censure in Luigi's voice, or was it just her imagination? It was her fault her young friends had taken such a severe battering.

The telephone rang again. Could it be Sandro, she wondered guiltily. Everyone had appeared to be in high spirits at the party, but perhaps this morning he'd had a change of heart; discovered she'd been responsible; was angry that his experimental work had been ruined. She nervously lifted the receiver. It was Roberto.

"Join me for breakfast," he said and hung up before she could reply.

Her fears compounded by the urgency in his voice,

Dotty dressed quickly. If she was in trouble, the sooner she faced up to it the better.

The moment she descended the hotel staircase her fears were instantly dispelled. The reception hall was a scene of frantic activity. Telephones were ringing incessantly. Luigi, usually alone at the desk, was being assisted by a couple of girls from the hotel's accounts office. They were all scribbling furiously on message pads, nodding their heads and smiling. As Dotty passed them, Luigi gave her a broad wink. No wonder his call to her had been brief.

Usually the breakfast room was rarely more than half full; guests trickling in a few at a time after their treatments as those who'd had the earliest appointments were just leaving. Today, however, all the tables were occupied and the muted murmur of voices replaced by a clamour of conversation and laughter. Even the waiters had a spring in their step. Roberto was half-hidden behind a newspaper he was reading, shaking his head in amusement. A pile of other newspapers lay untidily discarded on the table. He looked up as Dotty joined him.

"Is this all because of yesterday evening?" she asked, glancing around the room.

Roberto nodded. "What is it you say? Laughter is the best medicine? Nobody needs treatments today."

"But the mime troupe does," said Dotty, unable to

banish her concern entirely. "I'm worried that..."

"There is no need to worry, I know," he said mysteriously. "Now listen. You must hear what the *gran formaggi* have written about the performance."

"The what?"

"The big cheeses," replied Roberto. "The critics. They live in another universe." He scanned the review he'd been reading and translated for her benefit, speaking in an affected plummy voice:

"*It was a privilege to be a witness to the renaissance of the rich Italian comic tradition of improvisation etcetera, etcetera...It touched so many nerves,*" he added as Dotty giggled.

He picked up another newspaper folded over at the review. "This is my favourite," he said, stumbling over the translation.

"*The performance symbolised...the...exhausting, continuing physical and psychological demands artistes must overcome as they struggle to ascend the mountain of their art to reach the heights of recognition.*"

Roberto chuckled. "They are so self-important; so intense. They must always try to find a clever meaning. You should have seen the shock on their faces last night at the party when the hotel chef said: 'I just thought it was very funny. I laughed so much I cried!'"

"I suppose it doesn't matter what they write so long

as they liked it," remarked Dotty.

"*Si,*" said Roberto. "And Sandro will be a happy boy."

Sandro and company were lying on sunbeds around the pool in postures of sybaritic indolence. After weeks of roughing it on camp sites they were enjoying the temporary privilege of being treated as pampered guests thanks to the kindness of the hotel's management.

When Dotty appeared from the gardens, they heaved themselves up and limped and lurched over to her in a collective mime of the walking wounded; which would have fooled her into believing their injuries were genuine if their faces hadn't been alight with mischievous amusement. Nevertheless, a couple of the young people did have bandages on their arms.

"There is something I must tell you," said Dotty.

"We know," said Sandro.

"How did...?" she blustered, her colour rising; angry that Roberto who had counselled her, against her better judgement, to remain silent, had not only betrayed her but had told her not to worry.

"This is Italy," said Sandro grinning. "Everybody knows!"

"But how?" persisted Dotty, determined to get to the truth.

"Pietro was parking the van yesterday when he saw

you leaving the theatre with dirty marks on the knees of your trousers. He did not think anything of it at the time. But last night after the party when we were wondering who washed away the lemon juice he remembered and..."

"I only wanted to help..." began Dotty, her planned confession subsumed by shame at Pietro's lack of surprise that she'd been wearing scruffy trousers.

"It was fate," said Sandro. "If we had not met you I would have failed again. Pouff! *Un disastro.* People are calling the hotel asking for tickets; other theatres are asking for us as well. Luigi is going crazy! We rest today but we will give two extra performances in the Palladio and then we will leave to tour Italy."

"What about the conference this weekend?" asked Dotty.

"They are using the theatre only during the mornings," replied Fiametta.

Dotty indicated the bandages. "You can't take any more punishment," she said.

"No, no, it is OK," said Sandro, reassuring her. "We were not expecting to fall last night, but now we know what will happen we will fall properly. It will not to be so spontaneous of course, but no one will know." He looked at his watch. "Now, you must cancel everything. We are taking you out for the whole day. We want to thank you in a special way."

"Where are we going?" Dotty enquired.

"It is a secret," said Pietro.

"You will trust us?" asked Fiametta.

"Of course," replied Dotty.

"*Avanti* - come!" said Sandro.

Roberto, breasting the swimming pool, watched them leave; curious to know where they were going and hoping that Dorothea could get through the day without causing chaos. She might not be so lucky another time.

The group's minibus trundled through Bellarosa and onto the *autostrada*; Dotty in the front beside Sandro, Fiametta and Pietro in the back. The rest of the troupe had remained at the hotel. Later that morning they were to meet Luigi to sort through the enquiries from other theatres and plan a touring schedule.

The trio, conversing from time to time in Italian, kept glancing at Dotty, smiling like conspirators. She did trust them; but what had they planned for her, she wondered, as the kilometres mounted and they passed signs for Vicenza, Verona, and Brescia.

"*Eccola!* - here it is," exclaimed Sandro as they took the Milan exit from the *autostrada*.

"Milan?" queried Dotty.

"*Aspetti* - wait," said Fiametta, "It is not far now."

Dotty stared through the window in mounting anticipation as they sped through the suburbs and on into the centre of the city. Slowing down on one of the avenues leading to the cathedral, Sandro made a sharp turn between ornamental iron gates. Entering the shady courtyard of a severe grey-stone *palazzo,* its exterior softened by rampant ivy, he parked the battered old minibus beneath a towering magnolia tree. Dotty clambered out, stiff from her long journey on the hard, barely sprung seat in the old rattle trap. She fervently hoped the spa treatments would be back to normal the following day.

Sandro was skipping up the stone steps leading to the entrance of the building, Dotty following behind with Fiametta and Pietro. Although she'd been uncharacteristically patient so far, she was finding the continuing suspense almost unbearable. Spotting a highly polished brass plate fixed to the wall beside the entrance, she paused, hoping it might provide some clue:

"SALVATORE
ALTA MODA"

"Salvatore?" queried Dotty, something stirring in her memory.

"*Si,*" said Sandro proudly, glancing over his shoulder at her.

"*The* Salvatore?" she repeated, recalling her meeting with Madame Pompadour.

"You have heard of him?" asked Sandro, unable to disguise his surprise.

Dotty nodded, unwilling to explain further. She was already mortified by Roberto's, Pietro's and now Sandro's opinion of her lack of acquaintance with high fashion, and was damned if she was going to mention Madame's disdain.

It's like one of those stately homes we used to take Angela and Jenny to on wet weekends, she thought, intimidated by the grandeur of the entrance hall, with its black and white marbled tiles, glittering chandelier and mahogany double doors leading off on three sides; tall enough to allow a giant to pass through. She followed Sandro up an ornate staircase to the first floor, where he paused before yet another pair of mahogany doors. Whoever built this place, she observed, hadn't had to worry about Friends of the Earth nagging him about denuding the rain forests.

With a conscious flourish, Sandro opened the door. Stepping inside he held it open for the other three to enter; his eyes on Dotty in anticipation of her reaction to the Salon of Salvatore.

Dotty tentatively crossed the threshold of a pampered world of luxury, feeling like an interloper in her baggy cotton trousers and T-shirt; fearful that if she advanced further into the salon her scuffed sneakers would leave a trail of vulgar imprints in the thickly piled white carpet into which her feet had sunk. Her eyes widened as she took in the black leather couches, framed fashion sketches and catwalk photographs of models whose faces she vaguely recognised from magazines. There were no clothes in sight.

"Why are we here?" asked Dotty, swooning from the heady collective scent of a veritable Kew Gardens of long-stemmed white lilies arranged around the salon in enormous glass bowls.

"My friend, the one I tell you about who pays for my productions," said Sandro who'd been bursting to tell her his secret, "he is Salvatore. I live with him if you know what I mean."

"Good Lord!" said Dotty, instantly wishing she could have found more appropriate words in which to respond to his revelation. Such relationships were outside her experience, but as far as she was concerned, if it made Sandro happy - and it clearly did - then she was happy for him.

"He was not at the theatre," he continued, "He gets too nervous. Also people would recognise him. He stayed at home meditating; praying it would not be another disaster. But it was a triumph. He wants to say thank you."

"But..." Dotty faltered, remembering Roberto's warning about wanting to share the praise. "Why tell him? It was your efforts that made it..."

"I could not lie to him," said Sandro. "Salvatore is very good to me. I tell him the truth. That without you it could not have happened."

"By accident..." said Dotty

Sandro shrugged. "What is an accident? We have a saying in Italy: *Quando il momento e giusto* - when the time is right. You came along at the right moment."

"And you all made the most of it," said Dotty, as Salvatore made his entrance through an inner door. Catching sight of her, he momentarily struggled to maintain his professional smile but quickly recovered his composure. Good manners prevailed.

Dotty wasn't sure what she'd imagined he'd be like, but it certainly wasn't this. Short and stocky, with a shaven bullet head, bouncing across the room on the balls of his feet, he could have been mistaken for a prize fighter - except that no pugilist could have looked so sleekly elegant or retained unblemished such an impossibly noble Roman nose. It's extraordinary, she thought, swallowing rapidly, how celebrities seem to exude a kind of powerful magnetism that sets them apart from the rest of us.
Even his skin had an unearthly burnished sheen to it - as if he's been polished like one of Ronald's prize-winning apples.

"*Cara signora Lucas,*" he said, bending low and kissing her hand. "It is a pleasure to meet you. You have made us very happy. We have a little gift for you to show you our appreciation."

"I hope it's not a bunch of those lilies," Dotty

blurted out clumsily, "or I shall pass out." Very tactful, she thought, blushing furiously. You didn't have to make it so obvious you don't know how to behave in such rarefied circles.

She needn't have worried. Salvatore understood. Giving her the sweetest of smiles he wrapped an arm warmly around her shoulders. "I think you will enjoy what we have planned for you. Come," he said, ushering her towards the inner door.

Dotty turned enquiringly to Sandro.

"We will see you later," he reassured her.

A wisp of an elderly woman dressed in black was waiting for them. Introduced as Anna, she shook hands solemnly with Dotty, her warm brown eyes scrutinising her from top to toe.

"You will trust us?" Salvatore asked.

Dotty nodded, but wished they'd all stop saying that. It was sounding increasingly ominous.

"*Fa tutto* - do everything," he commanded Anna, understandably choosing not to translate his words for Dotty's benefit, before leaving the room.

Stripped down to her undies, she was relieved that childhood admonishments from her mother about being carted off to hospital in an emergency had ensured she had no bra straps fastened with safety pins. She stood patiently in front of Anna as she measured her. Although she spoke not a word of English, Anna communicated through gestures and appreciative nods of her head; far from being critical of *la signora's* body, she was filled with admiration that a woman of Dotty's age had kept such a youthful figure, and this all underpinned by an excellent bone structure. Dotty's self-confidence rose.

Handing her a pink cotton smock, Anna whisked her off to the floor above, where she was introduced to a pretty brunette called Tania;. Dotty's bundled up clothes and sneakers were promptly taken away. She's probably going to burn them, thought Dotty, her excitement mounting as she was ushered into a beauty salon.

Tania didn't speak English either, but once Dotty had understood that she should strip naked and climb onto the massage table, she had no desire to converse, only to surrender totally to what she sensed would turn out to be one of the most unforgettable days of her life.

Head resting on a pillow as soft as swan's down, massaged, exfoliated, moisturised, cocooned in towels as soft and thick as rugs, Dotty dozed in a state of disembodied bliss. Eyebrows plucked, eyelashes dyed, face tightening beneath a purifying mask of clay, the air thick with the intense fragrance of aromatherapy oils mingled with the astringent scents of lemon water and orange blossom, she felt as if she'd drowned in a vat of fruit salad and gone to heaven.

Staggering to her feet, pink-smocked once more, gently guided by Tania into the adjoining hair salon, she sank into a chair as Giacomo, with flowing locks, clad in leather trousers into which his legs must have been poured like plaster of Paris into a mould, appeared reflected behind her in the huge gilt mirror into which she was gazing.

Brows knitted, Giacomo lifted strands of her hair, sighing deeply, rolling his eyes to heaven, waking her from her reverie as he enacted that universal pantomime of Hairdresser's Horror. Any minute now, thought Dotty, amused, he's going to have an apoplectic fit and ask me why I allowed a gardener to take his shears to my head.

A sweet-faced young assistant washed and conditioned her hair, then separated individual strands with an eye-watering astringent gunk and wrapped them in tiny tin foil parcels. They're going to plug me in to an electric socket next, thought Dotty, and give me the shock treatment.

While her hair was cooking, a tray arrived with a delicious cold lunch: prawns and salad, grapes and parmesan, a glass of sparkling wine, and a delicate china cup of coffee. From time to time Sandro, Fiametta and Pietro popped their heads around the door to check on progress, called *"Ciao!"* and disappeared again grinning like gargoyles.

Dotty nibbled on a piece of cheese as a pedicurist

soaked her toes and a manicurist shaped and varnished the nails on her free hand. It was hard to believe that one body could keep so many people occupied. She was surprised that nobody had been appointed to pop grapes into her mouth, saving her the effort of feeding herself. All this attention was exhausting.

Foil parcels unwrapped, hair washed again, she returned to her seat as another handmaiden appeared. Placing a leather case on a small table beside her, she opened it to reveal an artist's palette of paints and powders and soft-bristled brushes. After studying Dotty intently, she mixed the colours like a painter and picked up a brush; Dotty staring in fascination as foundation, eye-shadow and blusher slowly but surely transformed her face.

Back came Giacomo. Wielding his scissors with lightning dexterity, he snipped and snapped at her head as Dotty, alarmed by the rapidly accumulating pile on the floor, wondered when he was going to stop. Brandishing a hair dryer, and to the sound of a small jet taking off, he whisked it over her head, using his other hand to brush and shape her hair.

"*Va bene,*" he said finally, satisfied. "You like?" he asked Dotty, switching off the hair dryer and stepping back.

Dotty more than liked: she was delirious with pleasure; turning her head this way and that as she admired the delicate feathering of the cut and the way the soft highlights shimmered as they caught the beams from the ceiling spots. Although she'd submitted to the team's ministrations without question, nevertheless she'd had a niggling fear that their collective efforts would make her unrecognisable: an artificial creation - like Barbie doll's mum. On the contrary, they'd contrived to subtly enhance what was already there. She was simply staring in wonder at a more beautiful version of herself.

"Grazie, Giacomo," she said. But she didn't need to thank him verbally. Her eyes said it all.

Accompanied once more by Anna, Dotty returned to the salon below where a new girdle, bra and the finest denier stockings were waiting. There was a dress hanging from a rail, the sight of which rendered her speechless. Anna was helping her into the dress as Salvatore joined them.

Dotty stood like a tailor's dummy as Salvatore straightened the skirt over her hips, and crouched down to adjust the line of the hem, rocking back on his heels as he cast a critical eye over her. Satisfied, he sprang to his feet.

"Perfetto.Un trasformazione assoluto perfetto" he pronounced, grinning broadly as Sandro, Fiametta and Pietro burst into the salon clapping their hands in

delight.

Dotty stood before a full-length triple mirror mesmerised by her own reflection, her insides bubbling like a magnum of champagne. Who was this woman wearing the midnight blue haute couture dress she'd last seen on the cover of Madame Pompadour's glossy magazine? On her feet were high heeled black pumps fashioned from the same moire silk as the lapels of the dress. On her beautifully coiffured hair was set the crowning touch: the black cocktail hat with its spray of peacock feathers, set at a jaunty angle, the veil raised. She wished with all her heart that the family could see her now.

"Cinderella, you *will* go to the ball!" Dotty exclaimed, aware that it had taken a lot more than a wave of a fairy godmother's wand to effect this transformation. But the team had worked magic nevertheless.

"Oh, Salvatore," she sniffed, trying to stem the tears that had sprung into her eyes, fearful of spoiling her mascara. "I can't believe it."

"Every woman is beautiful in her own way," said Salvatore gallantly, adding with understandable pride, "if she is given the right 'elp."

"But most women never get a chance to find out," Dotty replied, kissing him. "Thank you, thank you." She stared once more at her reflection, suddenly overcome by embarrassment. "You are the most exclusive designer in Italy. This must have cost..."

He patted her shoulder. "It is what we call the sample, *cara,*" he said as he appraised her once more with a professionally experienced eye. "You have kept your figure very well. *Complimenti.*"

Fiametta produced a camera and photographed Dotty alone, then with Salvatore and then, after Sandro had summoned everyone who'd been involved during the day, with the whole team. Bottles of *Prosecco* sparkling wine were opened and glasses were raised. "To Dorothea," they chorused.

"*A tutti* - to everyone. *Grazie!*" said Dotty, toasting them all.

I feel even more like Cinderella, she mused, after Salvatore's miracle workers had departed and she slipped behind a screen with Anna to reluctantly remove her finery. The clock's struck midnight and I'm back in my rags - except, she noticed, her cotton trousers and T-shirt had been laundered and pressed.

"This evening, Fiametta will help you to dress and to repair your make-up," said Salvatore as Sandro took the dress in its protective cover from Anna. Fiametta picked up a shoe-box and striped hatbox emblazoned with the name of Salvatore."I believe you have a surprise planned for a friend's birthday."

"How did you know?" asked Dotty.

As Sandro opened his mouth to speak she put up her hand to silence him. "Wait," she ordered, knowing he was about to utter what was fast becoming a catchphrase. "This is Italy," she said. She raised her arms like a conductor. "All together now..."

"Everybody knows!" they cried in unison.

"Wait a minute," said Dotty, her face falling. *"Everybody?"*

"Everybody except for signor Carducci," Sandro reassured her. "No one wishes to spoil *his* surprise."

He's going to get another one when he sees me, thought Dotty.

———————————

CHAPTER FIFTEEN

Here goes, thought Dotty in some trepidation, as she carefully placed one daintily shod foot on the top step of the hotel's sweeping staircase, praying she wouldn't lose her balance on the dauntingly slender high heels and finish up in an ignominious heap at the bottom. Down she went, head held high, one hand sliding along the balustrade, like the glamorous heroine in one of those Hollywood films of her youth who pretended to be oblivious to the upturned admiring faces of moustachioed cavalry officers and cigar- chomping dinner-suited men clustered in the hall below.

There was no need for pretence on this occasion. The hall was deserted. Never mind, I'll have to treat it as a trial run, thought Dotty, unaware that her descent had been observed by Luigi, who had just emerged from the reception office and was wondering whether a new guest had checked in while he'd been off duty.

The mystery was solved when Dotty approached the reception desk.

"It's me, Luigi," she said, giggling as she lifted her veil.

She's done it again, he thought. First the Ferrari, then the mime troupe, and now this. It's Italy. There's something about this country that transforms the most unlikely people.

"*Complimenti, signora Lucas,*" he said with genuine appreciation, "*molto elegante.*"

I could soon get used to this, Dotty thought, acknowledging the compliment. In the past she'd only ever been the centre of attention because of some mayhem she'd caused. It certainly made a welcome change to be noticed for her feminine charms.

"You speak lots of languages, don't you," she said.

Luigi shrugged modestly. "A few."

Dotty opened her evening bag and took out a slip of paper. "I've written something down in English. Please could you translate it and then help me to learn it by heart?" she asked, passing it across the desk.

"It would be my pleasure," said Luigi.

Before leaving with Sandro that morning, Dotty had arranged to meet Roberto in the hotel bar for an aperitif before dinner. Perched on a bar stool, nursing a Campari and soda, he glanced at his watch. She was late. Wondering whether Sandro's clapped-out old minibus had broken down, his attention was arrested by an expensively chic woman with a shapely pair of legs who was approaching the glass doors to the bar. Although her face was partly covered by a veil, she seemed somehow familiar to him. And yet...flirtation on his mind, he smoothed his hair in readiness.

Aware of being the focus of Roberto's intense scrutiny, Dotty clumsily caught the strap of her handbag on the door handle as she entered the bar and was forcibly yanked backwards. "Trust me to spoil it," she exclaimed, extricating herself in some confusion.

Non lo credo - I don't believe it, thought Roberto, recognising Dotty's voice. Stunned by the transformation, he slid from the bar stool and strode over to her as she lifted her veil. Gazing at her with undisguised approval, he took her hand and raised it to his lips.

"*Bellissima, Dorothea, bellissima!*" he said.

And probably thinking about time too, thought Dotty, thrilled by his admiration.

Pushing his Campari to one side, Roberto ordered a couple of Bellinis to mark the occasion, and settled down beside Dotty on a banquette to listen with obvious pleasure to her barely believable account of her day in Milan.

Finally, it was time to eat and as they left the bar, Dotty pulled the wisp of veil down over her eyes once more. Stepping onto the terrace, she was gratified to see Madame Pompadour's eyes feasting on what Dotty was sure she recognised as That Dress. Drawing level with the Frenchwoman's table, she paused, Roberto beside her.

"*Bon soir, Madame,*" Dotty greeted her graciously,

slowly raising the veil with one beautifully manicured hand as Madame stared at her, open-mouthed, desperately trying to regain her composure. Dotty silently counted to five and then continued, in word-perfect French: "*Je m'offre toujours un petit quelque chose de chez Salvatore chaque fois que je me trouve a Milan.*"

Having administered the *coup de grace,* Dotty calmly turned on her heels as Roberto nodded courteously to the Pompadours, and slipping her arm possessively through his, ensuring her red-painted nails were shown to their best advantage, crossed the terrace to their table aware that all eyes were upon them.

"I don't know what you said to poor Madame," he whispered once they were seated, surreptitiously observing the Frenchwoman through narrowed eyes, "but I think she is still in shock."

Dotty smiled. "I said," she translated in an undertone, savouring every word, "I always pick up a little something from Salvatore whenever I'm in Milan."

At the exact time Dotty and Roberto were enjoying plates of smoked salmon and Madame Pompadour was pushing hers to one side having lost her appetite, Jenny and Nick were arriving at the Pembertons for dinner.

"Where is she now, if I dare ask?" enquired Jenny accepting a glass of white wine from Paul.

"Still in Italy," said Angela.

"Mum's impossible. I got a postcard from her yesterday. Do you know what it said? *'Having a wonderful time. Glad you're not here.'* You'd think she'd miss her family," Jenny complained, ignoring Richard's smirk.

"It's the first time she's had a chance to get away from us all," said Angela. "She's enjoying every minute of it. Good for her."

"Mum, can't we..." interrupted Richard impatiently, indicating a parcel with an Italian postmark which had been delivered that morning addressed to the family and which Angela had insisted he delayed opening until they were all together that evening.

"I'm not sure I want to know what's inside," commented Paul as Richard opened the package and passed around the beautifully wrapped individual gifts it contained.

"Brilliant! Thank you, Gran!" cried Richard, who'd torn off the paper on his present to reveal what was obviously an expensive belt the colour of milk chocolate smelling richly of leather.

Looking considerably more hopeful now, Paul carefully untied the ribbon on his present only to have his hopes dashed when he unfolded a pair of white boxer shorts with *AMORE* printed across the seat.

Nick had received an identical pair; Angela and Jenny long T-shirts with the same word printed across the chest.

"Do you know what that means?" Richard asked his father, who was not joining in the laughter. "luurrvv!"

"I do hope you're not intending to wear that in public," said Paul to Angela.

"I thought I might wear it in bed," she replied, fluttering her eyelashes at her husband.

"Not in front of Richard," said Paul hurriedly, but nevertheless he looked pleased.

They had just risen from the sofas to move into the dining-room when the doorbell rang. Angela went into the hall to answer it. A distraught bespectacled figure, his trouser legs still held at the ankles by bicycle clips, stood on the doorstep.

"Is this the Pemberton household?" he asked with some urgency.

Angela nodded. Before she could react further Nigel had erupted into the hall and raced into the sitting-room.

"I can't cope. I just can't cope," he wailed. "It's all too..."

"Forgive me for interrupting," said Paul, "but who are you?"

"I'm sorry," said Nigel, registering their bewildered faces, "I forgot my manners. I'm Nigel Fairbrother.

Painless Travel. Mrs. Lucas's travel agent. She left me your address - reluctantly I might add - but I told her if there was ever an emergency."

"Emergency?" screeched Jenny.

"I thought I ought to let you know if you didn't know and..."

"Know what? What?" interrupted Paul harshly, trying to stem the manic flow.

"It's not my fault, truly," moaned Nigel. "She's such a determined woman."

"I think it would be helpful to all of us," said Paul, noting Angela's concern, "if you would kindly take a grip on yourself and explain calmly and succinctly why you are here. Perhaps you would like to sit down."

""Has Gran had an accident?" asked Richard, crossing his fingers behind his back.

"Not so far," said Nigel, doing as he was bid and collapsing on to the sofa.

"What do you mean 'Not so far'?" screamed Jenny.

"Now," said Paul, "what's happened to my mother-in- law?"

Nigel gulped. "She asked me to hire a Ferrari for her."

"This I would dearly love to see," said Nick with considerable relish, receiving a painful punch in the arm from Jenny.

"A Ferrari? You're not serious! Oh Gran's

amazing," said Richard, grinning with relief.

"But you refused to help her, of course," said Paul, frowning at his son's obvious approval.

Nigel opened and closed his mouth like a guppy. "Of course I did, *at first*," he said "but then...Mrs. Lucas is such a persuasive woman," he finished lamely.

Paul groaned. "I'm going to bring her home in a strait-jacket if it's the last thing I do," he said.

"Paul," said Angela in exasperation, "Leave Mum alone. Let her have some fun."

"Fun? Fun?" repeated Paul, his voice rising, his face red with anger as he rounded on Angela. "Do you know what a Ferrari costs? Can you imagine what the insurance premium must be? Your mother doesn't drive she...she ricochets."

"Oh Mrs. Lucas isn't going to drive it," said Nigel, foolishly imagining his words would ease the tension. "She said it was for an Italian friend to drive. To make his dream come true."

The colour drained from Paul's face. "This is all we need," he said. "Some swarthy young gigolo. Gold medallion. Hairy chest. Perfect white teeth. Probably sings."

"At first I said no and then, well, I was touched, really touched. It seemed so romantic. But I've just arranged for an air ambulance to collect a client who's been hit by a truck in Corfu, and I got nervous again and that's why I'm here." Nigel gabbled.

Jenny fixed him with a look of such malevolence that he shrank back into the sofa cushions. "I don't know why you were stupid enough to agree to it in the first place," she spat, "but if you've suddenly come over all conscience-stricken why haven't you just cancelled it?"

"It's being delivered this evening," said Nigel, "on his birthday. Mrs. Lucas said they'd go out in it tomorrow."

"Oh terrific," said Jenny sarcastically, "You have second thoughts when it's already too late. That's just brilliant."

Nigel's face crumpled beneath the onslaught of her attack. Angela glared at her sister. "If mum asked him to hire the car then he was perfectly entitled to do so," she said. "Nigel's a travel agent, not her keeper."

With a blood-curdling howl which would have terrified a Banshee, Jenny ran out of the room.

"I'm going to telephone her," said Paul. "Put a stop to this nonsense."

"That would be the proverbial red rag to a bull," cautioned Nick.

Although Angela was irritated by her sister's histrionics and doubtful about interfering, nevertheless the mention of a man being involved was disquieting. "How long is mum planning to keep the car?" she asked Nigel.

"Three days," he replied.

"Perhaps I'll go over; find out what's really going on," said Angela. "It would be nice to see Mum."

"I'll come with you," offered Richard, already rehearsing what he'd say to his school friends. "Just joining my Gran and her Ferrari in Italy for a few days."

"No you won't," said Paul, dashing his son's hopes. He turned to Angela. "If your mother's got involved with some cheap Romeo this needs a man - an Englishman - to handle it. Don't worry darling," he reassured her, misinterpreting her worried expression, "there won't be a fight, he wouldn't dare."

"I think you're going to need some help," said Nick, who'd been indulging his own fantasies. "If you're hoping to separate Mrs Lucas and her toy boy from the Ferrari you can't do it on your own. We're going to need a two-pronged attack here; and let's be honest about it, you do drive a Volvo."

"And what is wrong with a Volvo?" asked Paul, rounding indignantly on Nick,

Nick raised his hands in surrender. "Nothing," he said, "they're great, but I've always driven sports cars. Ferraris take some handling. Wouldn't do your image much good if you crashed it. You'll have enough on your plate keeping Mrs. Lucas and toy boy at bay. Someone will have to drive it back to wherever it came from." And, thought Nick, I'm going to make damned sure that person is me.

Although still smarting from Nick's remark, nevertheless Paul was man enough to acknowledge the sense of this. What about insurance?" he asked. "How will we..."

"No problem," said Nick. "In Italy it's the car that's insured not the driver."

"Well at least that's one thing less to worry about," said Paul, immediately realising it wasn't. "That means that if my mother-in-law wanted to..."

Nick grinned. "She could have a go behind the wheel."

Paul glanced at his watch. "Too late tonight, unfortunately," he said. He turned to Nigel, who'd remained hunched up on the sofa, twisting his hands nervously as he followed the discussion between the two men, his head going backwards and forwards as if watching a table tennis match. "Could you check if there are two seats on a flight first thing tomorrow morning?" .

Nigel opened his jacket and extracted a ticket folder from the inside pocket. "Always prepared is Nigel. Just got to fill in the names. I thought someone would probably want to go so I reserved two seats, just in case," he said, flinching as Jenny came back into the room and scowled at him.

"Thank you, Nigel," said Angela, "you've been most helpful."

"It would have been more helpful if he'd just refused to hire the damned car in the first place," said Jenny.

Angela frowned at her sister as Nigel rose. Whatever her mother's capacity for causing chaos, she'd shown great sense in trusting Nigel to organise her travels; and once she'd got the idea into her head she wouldn't have taken no for an answer. Nigel would have been no match for her. Even if he'd refused, she'd have pestered someone else until they'd given in from exhaustion.

"We're very grateful to you for trying to take such good care of Mum," she said, looking pointedly at Jenny. "I think you're wonderful!" Leaning down she gave Nigel a soft peck on the cheek.

Nigel blushed. "That's what Mrs. Lucas said before she set off," he replied "*And* she kissed me. You seem to go in for that sort of thing. It's not something my clients usually do."

"I'm sorry," said Angela, "I didn't mean to offend you."

"Oh that's quite all right," said Nigel. "I think I'm starting to like it."

Dotty's elation at the attention she'd received since her Milanese make-over was ebbing away as the time drew near for the promised arrival of the Ferrari. Would Roberto react with the same enthusiasm to the surprise *she* had arranged for him? Her stomach lurched as Luigi walked onto the terrace and headed for their table. He winked surreptitiously at Dotty before bending over Roberto and whispering something in his ear. Excusing himself, Roberto rose and accompanied Luigi from the dining terrace.

Unable to bear the suspense any longer, Dotty followed them at a discreet distance. Stepping into the reception hall, she positioned herself beside one of the tall windows facing the drive, half-hidden by a curtain.

Luigi was pointing excitedly at a luminous red Ferrari with a big blue bow on the top parked in front of the steps to the hotel's entrance. Roberto was looking alarmed: shaking his head in confusion, gesticulating wildly as Luigi, revelling in his discomfort, tried to reason with him.

With an almighty shrug which should by rights have dislocated his shoulders, Roberto spun on his heels and began to rapidly ascend the steps of the hotel. Tottering on her high heels like Minnie Mouse on speed, Dotty returned to the dining terrace. She had just resumed her seat when Roberto, looking thunderous, swept between the other tables.

"You buy or you steal?" he asked, sitting down heavily in his chair.

"I hired it - for three days," said Dotty.

Roberto made a gesture of dismissal. "Impossible,"

he said. "You cannot hire Ferraris in Italy."

"That's what Luigi said," replied Dotty, looking insufferably smug, "but there are ways. My travel agent arranged it with the owner - an Englishman, a retired racing driver who lives near Modena. He collects Ferraris."

"Huh. You think I can believe a man would lend a woman a Ferrari if nothing was going on between them?" retorted Roberto, infuriating Dotty with his misplaced Latin machismo.

"Of course you can. He's English," she reassured him, serving only to confirm the Anglo-Saxon male stereotype.

Roberto reached for the wine bottle and poured a healthy slug into his glass. "It's a funny old world," he mused. "Full of irony. An Englishwoman borrows Italy's best car from an Englishman for an Italian to drive. It is very funny." He wasn't remotely amused. "I am sorry but it is impossible for me to accept such a gift from a woman."

"I thought I knew you a little," said Dotty, dismayed at underestimating the depths of his masculine pride.

Roberto sighed dramatically. "No one can ever know me. I am too deep," he said. "The English, I do not understand them. I think mebbi they feel nothing with that stiff top lip then they go and do something crazy. You must send it back."

"Well thank you very much," said Dotty, finally losing patience. "for throwing my birthday present back in my face when I've gone to so much trouble and expense to arrange it. I've never heard anything so ill-mannered and ridiculous...and selfish. I would love to be driven in a Ferrari but because of your stupid pride you're happy to deprive *me* of the chance."

Roberto, subdued by her outburst, stared down at the table fiddling with his wine glass. "That is another point," he admitted.

"Anyway," said Dotty, "you won't deprive me. I'll take off on my own tomorrow. Drive it myself."

Roberto looked up in alarm. On the way to Verona Dotty had light-heartedly described her collision with Ronald's new greenhouse and admitted that driving slowly made her feel tired. He had a patriotic duty to protect his fellow-countrymen, and a longing to handle the Ferrari; loath as he was to admit it.

"OK. I try very hard to accept. Just to make *you* happy," he said, signalling the waiter and speaking to him rapidly in Italian. The waiter, amused, scribbled something on his pad and left.

"What was that about? Dotty asked, still reeling from Roberto's sudden capitulation.

"I've changed our order," he replied. "We will have steamed sole."

"Why?" she demanded.

"Because I am dieting," he said.

"Since when?"

"Since two minutes ago. If I am going to get into that *macchina* tomorrow a centimetre could make a big difference."

"*I* can get in," said Dotty. "*I* don't have to eat boring steamed fish."

"We must suffer together," said Roberto, grinning at her.

He's like a bear, she thought, one minute a grizzly, the next a teddy. She was still bemused by his change of heart. Why hadn't she stood her ground with Ronald? Why hadn't she tackled him aggressively about Bournemouth and the time he spent in his damned garden?; because she was married to him; had too much to lose to risk it. No, she recognised with sudden insight, for all Ronald's seeming mildness it wouldn't have made a scrap of difference. He wouldn't have changed his ways. Whereas Roberto, although going through the motions of not being seen to give in too easily, nevertheless did so - probably, she was honest enough to admit, when it suited him. Perhaps she'd unconsciously absorbed more of the Latin way of conducting relationships between the sexes than she'd realised. And the volatility certainly added to the stimulation of the game. She'd never felt more alive.

"We could go to Venice," she said. "But I suppose

it would be a bit silly unless a Ferrari floats."

"*Ma*, at the price it costs it should fly," he growled.

"Where should we go then?" she asked eagerly. "Let's make plans."

"First Rule of Life," he replied pompously, "never, never make plans."

"You said the first rule of life was never, never explain," cut in Dotty.

"OK," said Roberto, "*second* rule of life: never, never make plans. Who knows what may happen tomorrow?"

"But part of the pleasure is in the anticipation," Dotty protested.

Roberto shrugged. "*Va bene,*" he said smiling broadly. "Tonight you can make plans. Tomorrow I will decide."

"You really are very, very bossy," said Dotty, happily playing her part now.

Roberto raised his eyebrows in surprise. "A man must be bossy to control the woman." he said. "But I dunno, I think maybe you are uncontrollable."

After dinner they moved into the garden and sat on a bench, nursing brandies. As soon as the light faded, and as if responding to a celestial cue, out came the first fireflies of the year: thousand upon thousand of luminous fairy lights pulsing through the trees in the humid air like an overture to *A Midsummer Night's*

Dream. Dotty gasped in wonder, never having witnessed the phenomenon before.

Roberto watched her silent contemplation of the fireflies feeling his heart constrict; moved by her open response to the beauty of the night. She was not only *divertente e spiritosa* - entertaining and spirited - she was also a very good looking woman and a life-force to be reckoned with. He was ashamed of his earlier behaviour.

"I am sorry I was so rude," he whispered, reaching out and taking her hand. "It is the most beautiful birthday present I have ever received. Thank you. I am not accustomed to such generosity. You understand?"

"Yes I do," said Dotty. And she did.

Aware the night porter was following her progress, Dotty climbed the staircase as smoothly as she'd descended it earlier. Once out of his sight on the landing, however, she stopped. Steadying herself with one hand pressed against the wall she slowly and agonisingly prised first one foot and then the other from the high heeled shoes, groaning with tear-inducing relief as she wriggled her toes for the first time in hours. Swinging her shoes in her hand, humming *'I'm in the Mood for Love'*, she hopped, skipped and jumped her way in stocking feet down the corridor to her room.

CHAPTER SIXTEEN

The arrival of *la signora's* crazily imaginative birthday gift to Roberto had been greeted with universal joy by the staff. Temporarily abandoning their posts, deaf to the needs of the other guests, they were clustered around the Ferrari knowledgeably discussing its acceleration from rest to 100 k.p.h., its power output and top speed. Joined by Sandro and his troupe, they watched anxiously as Roberto familiarised himself with the controls; willing him to make a fine show of it. Masculine pride as well as national pride were at stake here.

Dotty, who had raced back to her room twice, having first forgotten her sunglasses and then her camera, was scooting across the hall when she bumped into Helga.

"I do not approve," Helga said.

"I'm very pleased to hear it," retorted Dotty. "If you approved of anything I did I'd know I must be doing something wrong."

"What about the damage to the environment?" she persisted, her obdurate single-mindedness impervious to insult.

"How did you get here from Germany?" Dotty enquired. "With your own wings?"

"We came together in a bus. Thirty people for one tank of petrol," said Helga with insufferable righteousness. "You should consider this."

"You may tink I vill but I von't," Dotty muttered under her breath as she ran down the steps.

"It's like the cockpit of an elephant," Roberto grumbled, frowning at the dashboard as she breathlessly joined him in the Ferrari.

"Elephant?"

"Big airplane. Fat nose."

"You mean a jumbo jet," she corrected him.

"That's what I said," he replied, staring at Dotty. "Where's all the paint gone?"

"Down the drain last night," said Dotty. "If I'd tried to make up like that this morning we wouldn't have left here before lunchtime."

"That is another point," he agreed.

"I'm sorry I'm not Sophia Loren," she said.

"She wouldn't get her bosom into this *macchina*," he replied, regarding her tenderly. "But it is not important, *cara.* You have a big, big heart."

He started the engine and the assembled spectators fell silent, listening to the car's characteristic snuffling notes with the same rapt expressions of appreciation as an audience listening to a *maestro* playing a violin concerto.

Everyone cheered and leapt back as the Ferrari took off with a squeal of rubber, almost demolishing a terracotta flower-pot before hurtling down the drive, spraying gravel in its wake.

Luigi winced as the car skidded to the left before shooting blindly out through the gates. He turned to the chef standing beside him. "*Forse sta'notte l'ospidale li troverebbe posti,* - perhaps tonight the hospital will provide accommodation," he murmured.

"*Spero di no,*" I hope not, the chef replied, crossing himself.

"If I do not learn how to control this tiger soon," moaned Roberto as they pulled up beside a toll booth at the entrance to the *autostrada,* "it would be safer to park somewhere and just sit on the grass and admire it."

Poking his arm out of the window in order to press the button to release a ticket, he was defeated by the shortness of his arm and the constriction of his safety belt. Twisting and turning, he became wedged against the steering wheel until, with one final heave of his body, he stabbed the button and snatched the ticket. Embarrassed by the traffic piling up behind him, he selected the wrong gear, the car bucked like a bronco, and the engine died. He tried again. The engine misfired and the car stalled once more.

The driver of a van next in line was leaning out of his cab and laughing so much at Roberto's inept handling of the car that he was in danger of choking.

"Three hundred million lire for a motor car which makes me look like an idiot," grumbled Roberto.

"Where is the dignity in all this?"

"You need longer limbs," said Dotty tactlessly.

"If I had longer limbs my feet would come out somewhere inside the bonnet," retorted Roberto as he whipped his head round and reacted angrily to something the van driver had yelled at him.

"What did he say to you?" asked Dotty.

"He wanted to know what happened to my little bicycle!"

Before he could stop her, Dotty leapt out of the car and marched up to the van, deaf to Roberto's desperate pleas.

"How dare you be rude to my friend," she shouted. "Just because you've got a dirty battered old van you...."

"*Mi scusi, signora, scusimi,*" the van driver said. Touched by her loyalty, he blew Dotty a kiss.

Somewhat mollified, she nevertheless gave the van a resounding kick before returning at a deliberately slow pace to the Ferrari, her progress accompanied by appreciative whistles and bleating of horns.

"Everybody has completely lost control of themselves," Roberto hissed as Dotty eased herself back into the passenger seat. "We are not a beautiful spectacle. We are a pantomime." With one of his disconcerting changes of tack, his face cleared and he looked at her with admiration. "I think mebbi you would kill for me, eh Dorothea?"

"Don't get carried away," she warned him.

Roberto pressed his foot hard on the accelerator and with a decibel-crunching howl the Ferrari surged onto the *autostrada*.

This is the life, thought Dotty, pushed back against the bucket seat by the force of the acceleration. Cars thundered down the *autostrada*. Articulated lorries shuddered and swayed, travelling at speeds far beyond their restricted limit. Then, on the inside lane, she spotted a Fiat just pottering along. Had she at last encountered a timid Italian driver, she wondered curiously, glancing across as they streaked past. An open book was balanced on the steering wheel!

"I've seen everything now," exclaimed Dotty. "That driver was *reading.*"

"Must be an intellectual," replied Roberto, unfazed.

The monotonously flat plains of the Po valley passed in a disorienting   blur as the Ferrari gobbled up the kilometres to Bologna. Not that it would have mattered if the landscape had merited their attention: the car was built for speed, not for watching as the world went by. Its sightlines were a driver's nightmare. Roberto, uncharacteristically silent and with both hands firmly on the wheel for once, was concentrating on what he could see - the road ahead.

Semi-recumbent and immobile in the cockpit, unable to see her feet or little beyond the window other than a smudged impression of massively pounding truck wheels looming above her, Dotty felt a sense of complete unreality. She wouldn't have been at all surprised if Roberto had pressed a button on the instrument panel and they'd taken off into outer-space. Forget about "better late than never," she thought, intoxicated by the raw sense of power and liberation the Ferrari transmitted, the truth is some things *are* definitely wasted on the young. Coming late to such experiences makes them even sweeter.

South of Bologna the countryside changed abruptly as the craggy peaks of the Apennines rose ahead. Ready for a change of scene, they left the *autostrada* at the next exit and took a winding route into the hills, their eyes adjusting to the change of pace as sunlight filtered through the surrounding foliage, shedding a shifting kaleidoscope of colours and shadows on the road ahead.

Roberto was in total command of the Ferrari now, skillfully negotiating the bends as they climbed higher, wearing an idiotic grin on his face as he listened to the organ chords of the engine. Passing through a necklace of small hamlets strung around the lower slopes of the Apennines, the car was greeted by smiles and whistles of appreciation from the local youth. It's like a royal progress, thought Dotty, only just stifling the impulse to wave regally.

Spotting a likely looking *trattoria*, Roberto pulled

over on the other side of the road. There was a sign to a car park behind the building and a couple of spaces in front.

"This is a difficult decision," he said. "If I park in front of the restaurant the *padrone* will see the Ferrari and add 20 per cent to the bill. If I leave it round the back it could be on its way to Yugoslavia before we've finished our meal."

"We'd look a bit silly arriving back at the hotel tonight by bus," said Dotty.

"That is another point," said Roberto, executing a sweeping turn and slipping into the parking space.

"Now this is what we do," he said as they entered the *trattoria*. "We do not talk to each other. We do not look at each other. We seem bored all the time."

"Why?" asked Dotty

"Because we have got to look like people who have been married for forty years, otherwise they will think you only come out with me 'cos I'm a rich boy with a Ferrari,"

The waiter spent rather a long time studiously removing non-existent bits of fluff from an immaculate snow-white tablecloth while Roberto studied the menu before ordering one course - again - for both of them.

"I'm hungry," Dotty complained as the waiter left.

"We'll eat tonight. When I think what that car has cost you we should be driving today, not eating," he replied as their waiter joined a couple of other members of staff who were standing by the window looking at the Ferrari.

"Well," said Dotty, "what do you think?" No giving is entirely unselfish, and she wanted to wallow in Roberto's delight in the Ferrari, as well as her own.

He shrugged. "You need an oil well in the garden to keep the petrol tank filled," he said, assuming a doleful expression. "It is very uncomfortable. I am glad I never bought one. It isn't even very fast."

"What a performance," said Dotty, "I don't believe a word of it."

Roberto grinned. "When you are happy you must not tempt Fate," he replied.

"And when you're miserable?" she asked.

"Ah, then you must pretend to be happy," he said.

They greedily crunched their way through an entire basket of breadsticks, ate a mushroom risotto, drank a couple of glasses of white wine and left.

"The problem is," said Roberto gloomily after he'd paid the small bill and they were walking over to the car, "the waiters will think we can only afford the Ferrari because we are starving ourselves."

"I do wish Air Traffic Control would get its act together," Paul grumbled to Nick, glancing at his watch ten minutes before they were due to land at Venice Marco Polo. "Taking off two hours late was bad enough, but I'd forgotten about the time difference. We won't land now until two-twenty."

Nick shrugged. "What's it matter," he replied. "Mrs. Lucas and the birthday boy will be hurtling around in their new toy. Best chance we'll have to catch them is at the hotel this evening. If you can persuade them to hand over the keys, we could drive the car back to where it belongs and return home on an early flight in the morning. We might as well sit back and enjoy the view. There aren't many approaches more beautiful than coming in low over Venice."

"I suppose you're right," said Paul as the intercom crackled and the British pilot regretfully informed them that owing to a collision - what he described laconically as "a slight disagreement" between a light aircraft and a refuelling bowser, the runway at Venice was closed and their flight diverted to Verona.

Paul groaned. "I don't need this," he said tight-lipped. "I should be at my desk, not chasing my demented mother-in-law around Europe. She's coming back with us, even if I have to chain her to my wrist!"

Nick grinned. "You shouldn't be so hard on her," he replied. "I like her. She's enormous fun."

"Fun?" repeated Paul. "Mother-in-laws aren't supposed to be fun. They should act their age; sit quietly by the fire embroidering tablecloths like my own dear mother."

Why am I not surprised, thought Nick.

Taking minor roads once more, Dotty and Roberto doubled back to Bologna for an *espresso* and an hour of sightseeing.

"Look," said Dotty, pointing at a road sign for Modena. "That's where the Ferrari came from."

"And where I hope it will return safely," replied Roberto, his unguarded remark belatedly and shamefully prompting Dotty to acknowledge that however pleasurable her gift, it had also burdened him with a heavy responsibility.

She had an opportunity to see most of Bologna from the window as Roberto, becoming increasingly fractious, manoeuvred the car through an obstacle course of ever narrower streets heavily congested with cars, Vespas and bicycles in a seemingly futile attempt to find a parking space. Finally, grumbling that it was easier to dock an ocean liner than the stiffly unresponsive Ferrari, he parallel parked in a just vacated space with less than an inch to spare.

In her eagerness to explore the city, Dotty was already half way down the street before Roberto had heaved himself out of the car. Wondering what was keeping him, she turned to see him walking towards her and, over his shoulder, a skinny boy sitting on the bonnet of the Ferrari. With a cry she pelted back past a surprised Roberto, grabbed the boy by the scruff of his neck, and yanked him off the car. Roberto joined them looking appalled.

"*Che cazzo la prende?*" the boy asked Roberto, rubbing his head.

"*E Inglese* - she's English," replied Roberto, reaching into his pocket and pulling out a small bundle of notes. Peeling off a couple he handed them to the boy.

The boy looked at Dotty and nodded, finding this explanation satisfactory.

"Why are you giving him money?" asked Dotty, outraged. "He was sitting on the car."

"I know," Roberto replied wearily," I promised him some money to look after the car. Now I have to give him some money in advance because you hit him."

Dotty looked suitably chastened. "I'm sorry," she said, "I didn't realise."

"Sometimes, I dunno," Roberto sighed, "I think you are a dangerous woman."

Paul and Nick found themselves in agreement when they emerged from Customs: neither of them wished to take the bus that the airline had laid on to transport them to Venice. Their solidarity wavered on the way to the car hire desk, when Paul muttered that if there was any justice in the world, his mother-in-law should pay for the hire car, and Nick countered that she hadn't asked him to interfere, and Paul then accused Nick of only coming along for the ride - in a Ferrari. Their disagreement was forgotten the moment they reached the car hire desk, where an assistant informed them that all bookings had to be made in advance and even if they had been prepared to make an exception, they couldn't, as it was only a small airport and they didn't have any spare cars.

Nick's mind was elsewhere. The desk clerk was a voluptuous young Italian woman with tousled raven hair. As Paul stubbornly refused to accept her protestations, she raised her eyebrows at Nick, who smiled. The attraction was instant and mutual.

"Where are you going?" she asked Nick, as a young male clerk appeared through a door at the back of the office.

"To Bellarosa," he replied.

"It's a matter of life and death," said a soulful Paul. "My dear mother-in-law is...is..." Seemingly too overcome to continue, he shook his head in sorrow as Nick looked on in astonishment.

"I am so sorry," she replied, instantly sympathetic. "I am just finishing for the day and meeting friends near Padova. I could take you there. Then you could find a taxi or a bus?"

"How very, very kind," said Paul. "Thank you."

Good old Mother Lucas, thought Nick, taking a sneaky peep at Luciana's long tanned legs as she changed gear, her mini-skirt the width of a bandanna.

If it weren't for her, he wouldn't be sitting here in a open-topped sporty number; the slip stream ruffling his hair; heading for the entrance to the *autostrada,* a crystalline sky above and a beautiful woman beside him at the wheel. What more could a man ask? Only that the glowering chaperone on the back seat would vanish in a puff of smoke.

"Ah guarda - look. I must buy some," exclaimed Luciana, pointing ahead to a farmer's roadside stall on a lay-by selling watermelons the size of cannon balls and once ubiquitous fiascos of wine in bulbous straw covered bottles which reminded Nick of his childhood. Rooting through his parent's attic during a school holiday, he'd come across a dusty pair, which his mother said she'd brought back from her honeymoon in Italy, and which his father had subsequently converted into table-lamps.

Travelling too fast as she approached the lay-by, Luciana swerved to avoid a mongrel which suddenly shot out from an overgrown farm track hidden by a stand of trees. Stamping her foot on the brake, she spun the wheel, missed the dog, but ploughed into the side of the stall dislodging a pile of melons and up-ending an open fiasco of red wine before coming to a shuddering halt.

Paralysed with shock and numb to the pain, Nick was pinned to his seat by a cascade of melons rumbling into the car like boulders in a rock fall.

Luciana was already out of the car, screaming curses and striding up to an elderly stubble-chinned farmer wearing faded bibbed dungarees and an old baseball cap, whose head had popped up from behind the stall.

Aware of an unnatural stillness behind him, Nick glanced in the driving mirror and was felled by an intense wave of nausea at the sight of Paul slumped in the corner of the back seat, apparently haemorrhaging to death.

He emerged from the car on jellified legs just as Paul, soaked from head to toe in red wine, his hair plastered to his scalp, wrenched open the back door, crawled out and collapsed onto the grass verge, looking suicidal.

I must not laugh, thought Nick, almost hysterical with relief as he looked down on a sodden, silent Paul. He turned his attention to the car. The impact had bent the front suspension and the wheel, with its punctured tyre, was touching the off-side wing. The car wasn't going anywhere unless it was behind a tow-truck.

Luciana appeared to have got the better of her argument with the farmer who, with a toothless smile, was pointing at Paul's soiled suit and then at his tin-can three-wheeled *Ape* parked beside the stall.

"You must go with the farmer," said Luciana with casual dismissal, taking out her mobile, "so your friend can be cleaned up. I will call my friends at the airport and they will arrange to collect me and my car. I am sorry. But what else can we do?"

Not a lot, thought Nick, disconcerted by Luciana's cool reaction to what could have been a very nasty accident. Such self-possession was unnerving and made him feel inadequate. He sent up a silent, guilty apology to Jenny for lusting after the Italian girl. Jenny doesn't cling, he told himself solemnly, she just needs me. And quite right too.

He exchanged muted farewells with Luciana and helped a meekly compliant Paul, still too out of it to protest, into the seat beside the farmer in the *Ape,* before clambering up himself to join the mongrel in the open flatbed behind the cabin. He wished Dotty a safe and happy day in the Ferrari as the *Ape* bucked and thumped its way up a seemingly endless unmade track more suited to an army assault course than an access to a farmhouse perched high on a hill.

Dotty and Roberto were standing on the pavement, staring with incredulity at an empty space that only a couple of hours earlier had accommodated a Ferrari.

"He couldn't have stolen it," said Dotty in despair. "He was just a child."

"Italians are *born* driving!" retorted Roberto "We will have to go find the police. Give me the documents."

Dotty opened her handbag and rooted around inside. Then she remembered. She closed her bag, unable to meet his gaze.

"I changed my handbag just before we left," she said.

"And the documents?" asked Roberto, "The letter from the Englishman?"

"At the hotel," she replied.

"It is against the law in Italy not to carry your documents," said Roberto. "Without them we have no proof that *we* did not steal the car."

"I didn't know that," said Dotty, looking contrite.

"*Va bene!*" said Roberto, struggling to control his anger. "We will return to the hotel. *You* will call this Forbes when we get back. *He* can report it to the police. It ...is...not...my...car."

"No," replied Dotty, refusing to be cowed by his icy fury. "But the chances are it was stolen by an Italian."

Roberto grinned. "That," he said, "is another point."

CHAPTER SEVENTEEN

"Very fetching," remarked Nick, as Paul shuffled into the kitchen naked except for an elephantine pair of faded bibbed dungarees belonging to the farmer's youngest son.

Paul gave him a murderous look.

Giuseppe, the razor-beaked patriarch, darting across the stone-flagged kitchen with a glass for Paul, reminded Nick of a bantam cock. Felicina, his wife, was a rosy-cheeked butter ball who barely came up to his chest. How could they have produced such a giant?

The couple spoke no English, Nick no Italian; but with expressive gestures and much sorrowful shaking of heads, they'd reached a mutual understanding while Paul was taking a bath, that his light-weight grey suit marinated in red wine, was likely to defeat even the most professional of dry cleaners. Felicina insisted, however, despite Nick's protestations, that she would at least try to remove the stains from Paul's white shirt and pants and launder them. She stretched the shirt over a bowl, sprinkled it with dry borax, then poured a kettle-full of hot water through it.

What kind of lunatic optimism, he asked himself, had induced them to assume that their mission of mercy would be completed within the day? Neither of them had thought to bring a change of clothes. It had occurred to Nick to ask Giuseppe to drive him into Verona to buy some casual clothes for Paul, but once they'd arrived at the farmhouse he'd been hit by a sickening delayed reaction to the accident: the shake in his legs subsiding only after a glass of Giuseppe's throat-stripping home-made brandy. And anyway, there appeared to be no vehicle in the farmyard other than the *Ape*. Even if they could have reached Verona before the shops closed, his bruises were beginning to throb and another jolting trip was beyond him.

Paul watched in some embarrassment as Felicina removed his shirt from the bowl and stretched his pants over it. "How long is this going to take?" he muttered helplessly. "You should have stopped her from doing...that...and just asked them to ring for a taxi."

Nick shrugged. "Apart from it looking discourteous when they've been so kind, I've no objection," he said. "I just assumed that as you have no choice but to go out into the world looking like Coco the Clown who's been left behind by the circus, you'd prefer to do so under cover of darkness."

"I dread to think what a taxi will cost from here to Bellarosa."

"The trouble with you," replied Nick letting his tongue run away with him, "is that you spend your entire life thrashing around in a futile attempt to control everything and everybody. You can't. It was your insane idea to come on this Mother Goose chase. Just think yourself damned lucky that we escaped with nothing more than bruises and a ruined suit."

"Don't lecture me," said Paul, lifting his tumbler of brandy with an unsteady hand.

The unwitting cause of the spat were sitting side by side on a wheezing local bus travelling along a country road to Bellarosa; but the distance between them was as wide and as cold as the Atlantic Ocean.

Roberto looked grim. "For the first time in forty years I am on an autobus," he said. "Me, a Roman. Where is the dignity in all this?"

Dotty, subdued, stared unseeing out of the window, not bothering to reply. She'd already been subjected to his complaints about the train they'd taken from Bologna to Padova. Sometimes, she muttered bitterly to herself, you do wonder why you bother. You try to bring a bit of sweetness and light into the everyday grind and you're assailed from all sides. If it isn't do-gooders tut-tutting in disapproval and blathering on about saving the planet, it's idle, envious parasites lying in wait to steal what you've worked so hard to afford. And if that weren't enough, the recipient of your generosity is so incensed that you forgot to bring along some stupid document that he sarcastically enquires whether you can still remember your own name.

Wishing the whole damned lot of them would go take a running jump off the nearest cliff, she was distracted by a young lad sitting across the aisle, who'd been eyeing them with amusement as they stiffly ignored one another and who now, unable to contain his curiosity any longer, asked Roberto: "*Qualcosa e andato storto?*"

"*Mi hanno portato via la Ferrari,*" explained Roberto through clenched teeth.

"What's so funny?" demanded a prickly Dotty as the boy laughed appreciatively at Roberto's reply; suspecting it had been at her expense.

"He asked me what was wrong, and I told him my Ferrari had been stolen," Roberto replied. He sighed. "I dunno. Even when you tell the truth in Italy nobody believes you."

Luigi looked up as the comically miserable pair walked wearily into the hotel in the early evening and approached the reception desk. He'd been waiting impatiently for this moment and was determined to enjoy it to the full.

Before they'd caught the train from Bologna, Roberto had had the sense to call Luigi to explain what had happened. In the unlikely event that the car was abandoned somewhere and found by the police, they would contact a none-too-pleased Forbes, whose own car documents were clipped to the driving mirror.

"The Englishman, signor Forbes, telephoned," said Luigi, "He has the car." He paused as they stared at him in astonishment.

"But...but I don't understand," said Dotty finally, looking relieved.

"Parking on the street in the centre of Bologna is limited to thirty minutes," said Luigi, shaking his head in mock sorrow at Roberto, who should have known better than to risk outstaying his welcome. "So it was carried away on a truck by the *Vigili* - traffic police - and taken to the car pound."

"*You* should have thought of that possibility," said Dotty, rounding on Roberto.

"What difference would it have made," he countered. "Without the letter of confirmation from the Englishman they would not have released it."

"But how did Mr. Forbes know?" she asked, returning her attention to Luigi.

"The man in charge of the pound," Luigi explained, "is a motor racing *afficionado*. Modena is close by. He recognised the name on the documents. He was curious to know why, after some hours, nobody had enquired about such a valuable *macchina*. So he telephoned signor Forbes, who telephoned the hotel. When I told him you were returning here, he drove to Bologna with a friend to collect it. I promised to return your set of keys."

Roberto, emitting a huge sigh of relief, handed the Ferrari's keys to Luigi. He turned to Dotty. *"E un teatro, la vita, eh cara?"* -life is a theatre!

She nodded. "What a day" she said, relaxing at last.

"A fantastic day," he replied. "Thank you. You are a crazy woman. I shall never forget."

They'd returned too late for dinner, but before they went to their rooms to shower and change, Luigi said he'd ask the kitchen to rustle up a platter of cold meats and salad. Now, their meal over, the other guests long gone to their beds, chairs stacked on tables all but their own, they were dancing on the deserted terrace to lush string orchestrations of Neopolitan love songs; the music coming from Roberto's cassette machine sitting on the bar.

"By the way," he murmured, "My birthday isn't until next Thursday."

"I know," replied Dotty, his remark forcing her finally to confront what she had desperately tried to ignore for the past nine days. "But I'll be in Spain on Wednesday.

"And I leave for Rome very early tomorrow morning," said Roberto, feeling Dotty stiffen in his arms.

They remained silent, knowing they were sharing

the same thought: that neither of them, until this moment, had dared to mention the date of their departure.

"But..." Dotty said, puzzled, "You knew I'd hired the Ferrari for three days."

"I did not want to spoil today," replied Roberto. "And anyway," he added, trying to lighten the mood, "I hoped mebbi when I had gone you would send it back."

But rather than lighten their mood, the revelation that this was their last evening together intensified it. This is the first time since Ronald died that I've been so physically close to a man, thought Dotty, nestling against the comforting masculine bulk of Roberto, feeling the pressure of his hand on her back, the softness of his cheek, as he guided her around the terrace. And it's more than just a need for cuddles, she acknowledged, suddenly overcome by shyness as she inhaled the lemony scent of his aftershave. I'm aroused. I haven't felt like this for a long time."

Luigi and the barman, about to go off duty, glanced across at the terrace. "*Forse, ci trovarebbe una camera libera sta notte*" - maybe we have one room unoccupied tonight - observed Luigi, as they left the hotel.

The music ended but Roberto held on to Dotty. Turning her head towards him, he kissed her tenderly. It was a long, satisfying kiss. Unable to meet his eyes

- 219 -

as he released her, Dotty buried her head in his shoulder.

"Again?" he murmured into her hair.

She nodded. It was even better the second time.

"I think I will finish my drink down here alone," he whispered. "And then, mebbi I could pass by if you are not asleep?"

He's still drunk, thought Nick, glancing over his shoulder at Paul sprawled across the back seat of the taxi as it pulled up outside a *pensione* in Bellarosa, which Giuseppe had telephoned to make a reservation for them. It would have been impossible for Paul to enter a restaurant without attracting ridicule, so they'd accepted Felicina's generous invitation to join them for dinner. Paul, to Nick's amusement, had grievously underestimated the strength of Giuseppe's walnut liqueur.

On the journey to Bellarosa he'd awoken from his stupor and insisted with the belligerence of the inebriated that Nick could stay wherever he liked but that he, Paul, was going on to the Hotel Palladio. After the day they'd had, who knew what the Furies had lined up for them the following morning. He was going to stay where his mother-in-law was staying and that was the end of it.

Nick was too tired to care any more what Paul did. He'd called Jenny on his mobile and lied that all was well but that they'd been delayed, and asked her to pass the message on to Angela. He'd even had the sense to jot down Paul's measurements. Getting out of the taxi, he paid the driver then opened the back door and nudged Paul.

"I'll buy you some clothes early tomorrow and bring them to the hotel," he said.

"'Tank you...mo... most grateffful..." murmured Paul before drifting off once more.

Nick stood on the pavement and watched as the taxi drove off. What if the hotel didn't have a room free? To hell with it, he thought. It's not my problem.

Dotty entered her room, turned her key in the lock with a shaky hand and leaned back against the door, her heart pounding like a tom-tom. Having married young and been closeted within the confines of a faithful marriage, she was not equipped to cope with this. She'd only known Ronald - in the biblical sense. If a man found her desirable the inevitable suggestion would be made. If it hadn't been, should she have felt relieved or insulted?

Could she separate sex from love? She wanted Roberto, she couldn't pretend otherwise, but could she give in to desire without commitment? Did it produce pleasure or a distancing of emotion? Was an honest *no* better than a dishonest *yes;* allowing herself to be seduced because she didn't want to hurt the man's feelings by refusing?

She paced the room in a state of considerable agitation, twisting her wedding ring round and round on her finger. Would he want to stay the night? What if she snored? What were the conventions of waking up in the morning beside a man who, however demonstrably affectionate and companionable, she didn't really know?

Was her new freedom a licence to fall into bed with a man she fancied or the responsibility to choose what was right for her? And how would she know unless she tried it? What if Roberto's repertoire was, well...more imaginative than Ronald's? If she went to bed with him and he was enjoying it but she wasn't - could she stop him half-way through? Say 'thanks very much but I've changed my mind'? On the other hand, she thought, her face flushing, who knew what previously unknown pleasurable sensations she might experience?

She snatched open the drawer of the beside cabinet and removed Ronald's photograph. Sinking onto the bed, she stared down at his comfortable old face.

The reception area was softly lit. Gianni the night porter was slouched in a chair behind the desk, watching a small portable television. He looked up as the entrance doors crashed open. Blinking rapidly, unable to believe what he was seeing, he gazed in enchantment at the man who'd staggered in dressed in a spotless white shirt and outsize bibbed dungarees with drooping upturned cuffs exposing a pair of English brogues. To set off the magical ensemble, he'd added a crumpled and stained striped tie.

Gianni watched expressionless as Paul slowly crossed the hall, carefully placing one foot in front of the other with the exaggerated care of someone walking on a tight-rope. Roberto, coming in from the terrace, was stopped in his tracks.

"Where...is...shhee?" Paul burbled, clinging on to the reception desk. "I must find her, Mishus Loocas and... ro-romeo."

Hearing Dotty's name, Roberto, took a quick step backwards and disappeared from sight.

"She's my mother-in-law, you know. A respectable old lady who's been taken advantage of by a gigolo," confided Paul in a sudden articulate rush, as Roberto's disembodied head appeared around the terrace door. Unable to resist the temptation to get closer, he padded silently like a cat into the reception hall and hid behind a pillar.

Gianni's face was set in stone. Registering this, Paul's normal good manners struggled to the surface. "Not...of course, that I...I blame him. If you want to know the truth... she's a...a delinquent. Gadding about Europe...She's taken years off my life, you know," continued a maudlin Paul, tipsy tears welling in his eyes. "She's comin' home wiff me...where she belongs."

Roberto involuntarily nodded his approval of such a sentiment.

Dotty's eyes frantically scanned the room, coming to rest on the rose Roberto had tossed up to her on the night of their balcony scene. He was leaving in the morning. This was her last chance and, she finally admitted, her resolution faltering, she ached for him. Was he giving her time to prepare? Did he expect her to be undressed? Would it look forward if she greeted him in her nightie? Quite the opposite, she thought. Her ankle-length chain store cotton buttoned-to-the-neck made her look more like Wee Willie Winkie than a passionate seductress. He'd take one look and plead a sudden headache.

Be honest, she told herself. Morality has nothing to do with your indecision. Nor has physical vanity - Roberto's seen you without make-up, in a swimsuit and he still wants you. It's your fear that you'll be found wanting in bed; that you might not come up to scratch. So what. At your age it's not the things you do that you'll regret but the things that you don't do. Since when have you been afraid of trying anything once?

Tip-toeing over to the balcony she looked down. The terrace was deserted. Roberto must be on his way. Picking up Ronald's photograph she slid it back into the drawer, ran across to the door in stocking feet and unlocked it. She returned to the balcony and turned to face the room, her back pressing painfully against the rail as she waited for Roberto, swaying slightly on her feet like a swimmer poised on the edge of a diving board before plunging head-first into the deep end. The telephone rang. Startled, she crossed the room and lifted the receiver with a trembling hand.

"Signora Lucas?" said Gianni. "There is someone to see you in reception. It is urgent." He hung up before Dotty could reply.

Breathless with panic, she ran, shoeless, down the corridor. Who could it be? Had something happened to one of the girls? If it had, surely no-one would have come in person to tell her - unless the news was too tragic to convey by telephone...? She paused at the top of the stairs and gazed down. Her son-in-law, looking like a grotesque caricature of himself, waved at her with an unsteady hand. Fearing for her sanity, momentarily convinced that he'd materialised out of her niggling guilt that making love with Roberto would be a betrayal of the family, Dotty slowly descended the staircase.

Dotty stood by her bed, gazing down at Paul, the room reverberating with his snores. The hotel was fully booked. In his condition, it would have been impossible to send him away. Where could he have gone at this time of night? Taking the rose from the glass on the bedside table, she stumbled across to the balcony on leaden legs. In a gesture of confused loss and resignation she let go of the rose and watched it fall.

Roberto, hidden in shadows below, trying to quell his own disappointment with wry amusement and a philosophical acceptance of the tortured twists of fate, was also watching as the rose fell.

Gazing down at its petals strewn like confetti at his feet, he didn't move until he heard the click of shutters closing.

For one last time, he looked up at the balcony. *"Buona notte, Giulietta,"* he called softly on the night air. "They don't make them like you no more."

CHAPTER EIGHTEEN

Not quite the morning after I'd imagined, thought Dotty, or the night before. She rose stiffly from the chaise-longue where she'd slept. That damned Ferrari. Given half a chance she'd strangle Nigel.

Sunlight filtered through the shutters casting slanting beams across the bed and her still snoring son-in-law. As to why someone as abstemious as Paul should have arrived legless and wearing such a preposterous assortment of clothes was beyond even her fertile imagination. It had been impossible to get any sense out of him the previous evening. She was surprised that rather than feeling angry at his intervention, she felt an intense maternal tenderness towards him. It was the striped cricket club tie that did it. Whatever had caused him to lose control, to behave so out of character, she sensed that the tie had been his endearing attempt to hang on to his dignity. He was a pompous idiot protective of his own reputation but she also knew, in her heart, that he genuinely cared for her; however clumsily he expressed it.

When he woke, he was going to be painfully embarrassed, particularly in her presence. Creeping around the room, gathering some clothes together, she dressed quietly in the bathroom and then slipped out of the room.

I'm losing my grip on reality again, thought Dotty, clutching the balustrade of the staircase as Nick, looking remarkably jaunty and carrying a couple of large plastic bags, strode into the hall.

She grabbed his arm for reassurance. "Is it really you?" she asked in a shaky voice. "Tell me I'm not hallucinating."

Nick grinned. "It's me alright," he said. "Where's old Bib and Braces?"

"In my bed," replied Dotty. "Still out cold."

Nick held up the bags. "New trousers, shirt, shaving stuff. Shall I put him out of his misery before I tell you all?"

"Good idea," said Dotty. "Room 16. Join me for breakfast."

Aware that Luigi had been watching them with interest, she crossed over to the desk. She could hardly bear to imagine what kind of a scene Paul had made the previous evening before Gianni had called her.

"I'm so sorry about what happened," she said. "I hope the other guests weren't disturbed. I'd no idea that he..."

Luigi was sympathetic. "Unfortunately, we had no free rooms," he said. "So..."

"I'm very grateful," said Dotty distracted by a dejected Professor Albrecht slowly descending the staircase, clutching a sheaf of papers. "It's not like the Prof to be so miserable," she commented.

"It is very bad," said Luigi. "A special moth he found in the woods has disappeared. Now he cannot discuss it at the final day of the conference tomorrow."

Their eyes met. They shared the same unspoken suspicion of who was the likely culprit.

"Well?" asked Dotty as Nick rejoined her.

"I wouldn't want his head on my shoulders this morning," said Nick "He looks like Doctor Death."

Luigi, amused, said he'd ask Room Service to send up a litre of orange juice and a very large pot of black coffee.

Over breakfast, Dotty told Nick about the Ferrari's premature departure and Nick described in graphic detail to a disbelieving and captivated Dotty the events that had led up to Paul's inebriated arrival at the hotel.

"Before he appears, there's something I must tell you," said Nick, as Dotty wiped tears of mirth - and relief that they'd escaped unharmed - from her eyes. "I called my agency this morning, and there's bad news and good news about your house. The bad news is that the sale has fallen through - the purchaser won't be able to complete. His company has gone into liquidation. The good news is that as you'd exchanged, the contract is legally binding and the deposit non-returnable, so you've made yourself thirty thousand pounds even before we put the house back on the market."

Dotty stared at Nick open-mouthed. "You can't be serious!" she said, finally.

"Oh yes I am," he replied. "Legally you could demand the entire amount, but there's unlikely to be anything in the kitty."

She shook her head. "Certainly not!" she said.

"But it does mean you'll have to come back for a while," he went on. "Now we're starting all over again, the garden will have to be made presentable and the house smartened up a bit. Still, you can afford it now."

"I won't have to do all that smells of bread baking and real coffee routine, will I?" asked Dotty.

Nick grinned. "No need to go to those lengths," he replied. "Now," he added, looking serious. "There are a couple of other matters I'd like to discuss with you - in complete confidence."

I can't take all this in, thought Dotty ten minutes later. "I'm thrilled," she said, squeezing Nick's arm affectionately. "And as for your idea - it's absolutely brilliant."

"Once it's all sorted out," Nick assured her, "you can set off on your travels again."

Dotty wasn't so sure. After the emotional roller

coaster of the past twenty-four hours and now Nick's revelations, the desire to travel had lost its urgency.

"By the way," she said, "Let's have no more 'Mrs. Lucas'. I'm Dotty."

"I know you are," ventured Nick, "I appreciate it."

Paul was waiting for them in reception. Clad in the new chinos and blue shirt he looked like the old Paul until he slowly ratcheted his head round at their approach and regarded them with blood-shot eyes.

"It was inexcusable that you had to spend the night on the couch. I'm so very sorry for what happened," said Paul.

"The matter's closed," said Dotty, kissing him on the cheek. He'd suffered enough. "I no longer have the Ferrari, and as for your adventure yesterday - it'll remain a secret between the three of us. Mum's the word."

"Thank you," said a contrite Paul. "I'm most grateful."

"I still have some unfinished business here," she said, "but tell Angela I'll be coming home in a couple of days or so."

"I hope I haven't...." said Paul.

"It's nothing to do with last night," Dotty reassured him. "Nick will explain." Although there was no reason why the rest of the family shouldn't be told about the sale of the house falling through, she'd agreed with Nick that the other matters they'd discussed would not be divulged for the time being.

As for that unfinished business, she thought, once the men had left for the airport, I'm determined that Professor Albrecht will have his Red Underwing moth for the last day of the conference. But other than stretching Helga on the rack in the hope of extracting a confession, what could she do? Mulling over her past conversations with the Professor, searching for clues, she was about to reluctantly admit defeat when she remembered something a friend had told her about an eccentric spinster aunt. Of course! It would require some careful planning, but it might produce results.

Few of the shop assistants in Bellarosa spoke English and, she was ashamed to admit, made lazy by Roberto's and the hotel staff's command of her own language, she'd barely glanced at her Italian phrasebook since her arrival. But her shopping list would be long and complicated. To ensure there would be no time-consuming misunderstandings, she borrowed an Italian-English pocket dictionary from Luigi and after an hour of concentrated mental effort, she set off for Bellarosa impressed by her efficiency.

She was just about to complete her purchases in the stationery shop when Sandro walked in, kissed her warmly on both cheeks, and raised his eyebrows at the curious collection of items laid out on the counter.

Over a cappuccino, Dotty outlined her plan.

"*Fantastico!*" he exclaimed. "*Perfetto!* It is a wonderful idea. But you cannot do this alone. We will help. Meet me after the performance this evening. I will bring some other things I think we will need."

Dotty's sudden riches, the saga of Paul and Nick's visit, and her soon to be realised plan which she hoped would save Professor Albrecht, had kept her thoughts occupied during the day; thankfully giving her little time to dwell upon Roberto's departure. But now, sitting over a solitary dinner, painfully conscious that those hazel eyes were no longer regarding her with affectionate amusement across the table, his absence was almost too much to bear. Your misery won't bring him back, she told herself. Be grateful for the time you spent together.

Easier said than done, she thought, as she took a stroll in the gardens before returning to her room. She changed into a pair of black cotton trousers, an old T-shirt and a pair of sneakers. Finally, under cover of darkness, it was time to go. She took the lift down to the treatment rooms and left the hotel undetected, by the back door.

Fiametta, said Sandro when she joined him and Pietro behind the theatre, had not taken part in the performance that evening and was not free to join them, being occupied elsewhere. He reassured Dotty that she was well, but seemed unwilling to explain further. The men were dressed in black from head to toe and Sandro, nodding in approval at her black trousers, handed her a baggy black polo-necked sweater.

In addition to the carrier bags containing her shopping, which Sandro had insisted he should carry back separately from Bellarosa, fearing the porter might try to relieve her of them on her return to the hotel and thus arouse suspicion, he'd added a couple of his own. To Dotty's glee, he had secretly "borrowed" the three motorised scooters that were kept in the spa annexe for less mobile guests.

"To the Woods!" cried Dotty, clambering onto her machine. With carrier bags balanced precariously on their knees, they set off in single file along a narrow path which circumvented the gardens and led to the woods. Unpacking the bags in an abandoned summer-house, they set to work assembling their moth-hunting equipment.

"OK," said Sandro as they put down their brushes. "We are ready now."

Attired in brown paper capes and cardboard hats all painted with a mixture of rum and molasses, their faces hidden behind black masks; they picked up their specimen jars containing chloroform-soaked cotton wool, and, with lanterns held high above their heads, skipped joyfully into the woods.

Sandro held up his hand, signalling they should pause. "Follow me," he whispered. "We will take this path further into the wood so the trees will shield our lights from prying eyes. Then we will wait."

Dotty and Pietro dutifully followed their leader until they arrived at what appeared to be a natural clearing in the woods. Like cowboys waiting for the Injuns to attack the wagon train, they stood silently in a circle facing outwards.

"Now we will cast a spell," said Sandro. "All together now. Say after me: "Come! Come beautiful moths!" he intoned like an incantation. "Help the *professore.*"

"Come! Come beautiful moths!" the trio repeated in unison. "Help the *professore.*"

Unlike butterflies, moths used the moon to navigate and were easily confused by anything else that shone in the dark. And here they came - gauzy mottle-hewed clouds of them drawn magnetically to the lantern light and the sweet-smelling goo; flapping and fluttering, sticking to Dotty's cape and hat until she was smothered with the delicate beauties.

Dotty was bewitched; transported into the delicate colour-washed illustrations of her daughters' childhood books of myths and fables: a wonderland of sylvan glades, Pan and Puck, wood nymphs, elves and fairy queens. Swirling and twirling, swinging her lantern, she was unaware she'd become separated from Sandro and Pietro until, rudely awoken from her dream-like state by the sound of heavy feet thrashing through the undergrowth, she paused, and lookng around her in dismay, realised she was alone.

Peering through the trees, searching for the comforting glow of their lanterns. she was blinded, without warning, by the beams of powerful torches. She froze, mouth wide in terror, as menacing black-clad figures armed with machine-guns rose from the undergrowth and surrounded her.

Dotty sat on a truckle bed in her immaculately clean police cell and stared at the locked door. She was in the slammer. The cooler. The calaboose. What a come-down. One day you're zooming around in a Ferrari, wearing haute couture, wondering whether to go all the way with a handsome Italian admirer, the next you're in clink doing porridge. When would she ever learn to control her impetuosity?

But she'd only wanted to help dear Professor Albrecht. Why should she be punished when someone like Nelly, with criminal intent, kept getting away with it? Where was the justice in that? And since when had it been a criminal offence to go hunting for moths? Why hadn't they put everyone at the lepidopterist conference under arrest? And where were Sandro and Pietro?

As for the *Carabinieri*: those machine-gun toting, impossibly good-looking Elvis Presley look-alikes with melting eyes and impeccably tailored toy town uniforms, smoking cigarettes and strutting around like male models in their tight trousers! How could she concentrate on their questions when she was waiting to hear someone shout "Lights. Camera. Action!" Of course she couldn't give them proof of her identity. Did they really expect her to be carrying a passport beneath a moth-smothered smock? So now she was locked up until someone could confirm she was who she'd protested she was.

Still, it would only be a brief incarceration, she reassured herself. The officer in charge had told her the British Consul would be informed. Once he got to hear about it she'd be a free woman again in no time. A tall, distinguished man in a pinstripe suit, looking like David Niven, would arrive in a Rolls Royce with the Union Jack flying and carry her off.

But as the hours passed with no word from anyone she became increasingly despondent. Where was the Consul? Still swanning around at a diplomatic reception stuffing himself with Ferrero Rocher chocolates, no doubt; while one of Her Majesty's subjects was left rotting in a rat- infested dungeon. Well not quite, she had to admit. It was a very clean cell, but the principle was the same.

To keep up her flagging spirits, and in the hope of

attracting someone's attention, she stood by the cell door and treated the lock-up to a tuneless but rousing rendition of patriotic songs - "*Rule Britannia!*" "*There'll always be an England*" and "*Land of Hope and Glory*", - giving particular emphasis to the words '*Mother of the Free.*' Sadly, the only response came from a disembodied male voice yelling "*Silenzio, Signora!*" So much for our liberating Europe, she thought. What short memories people had. Where was the gratitude?

She suddenly felt very alone. Pull yourself together, she told herself. She'd show them. The sooner she went to sleep the sooner she could face up to whatever the new day would chuck at her. In the morning they were going to look very, very foolish.

CHAPTER NINETEEN

She'd just risen from her truckle bed when the cell door opened and a policewoman brought in a tray bearing breakfast; or rather the continental travesty of what passed for a breakfast, thought a ravenously hungry Dotty, suddenly overcome by homesickness as she imagined the joy of tucking into a plate of bacon, eggs and fried bread.

"How much longer are you going to keep me here?" she asked.

The policewoman spoke no English but understood her concern. Patting her on the shoulder she smiled sympathetically then left, locking the cell door behind her. Dotty stared at the breakfast tray. Better keep my strength up, she thought bravely, picking up a bread roll.

When the policewoman returned to remove the tray, she was not alone. A tall, distinguished man in his early fifties, wearing a pinstripe suit, his abundant pepper-and- salt hair rising above a noble forehead, strolled into the cell with loose-limbed elegance.

"Mrs Lucas?"

"That's me," said Dotty, her face glowing with relief.

"Charles Whittaker. British Consul," he said as they shook hands.

"I've never met a British Consul before," said

Dotty, clinging on to Whittaker's hand as she gazed up adoringly at him, "but you're just how I imagined you'd be."

"You're too kind," murmured the Consul, although her guileless remark had not been unexpected. However egalitarian the Foreign Office was these days, he was well aware, not without a touch of vanity, that for Dorothy Lucas and other women of her generation, he was the very model of an old school British diplomat: Carlton Browne of the F.O personified.

Mrs. Lucas, however, did not conform to his previously held assumptions about respectable suburban ladies of a certain age - stalwarts of the W.V.S. and W.I. – who occasionally required consular assistance. He was more accustomed to replacing their stolen passports or advising their relatives on the procedure for shipping their bodies back to the UK following a heart attack than he was visiting them in detention.

"Right," said Dotty striding towards the cell door. "Let's go!"

"Not yet, I'm afraid," said the Consul, putting out a restraining hand and indicating she should sit down. "Before having a word with the *Marasciallo* - the officer in charge I need to know exactly what happened."

He maintained a diplomatic silence and with

considerable difficulty a straight face as Dotty breathlessly recounted the events leading up to her arrest and her involvement with Professor Albrecht, Helga and the mime troupe.

"I was only trying to help," she explained, "and I have my own suspicions about who tipped off the Law."

He smiled. "It would appear that there's been a been a misunderstanding," he commented. "I'll make some further enquiries and get back to you as soon as I can. Don't worry. I'm sure we can sort this out."

Dotty watched the Consul leave, secure in the conviction that this Knight in Shining Armour would rescue her from the tower. To pass the time, she recited those evocatively imperial words printed on the inside cover of the now sadly defunct blue British passports: words long ago imprinted on her memory from when, feeling low, she'd taken down the dusty hatbox on top of the wardrobe and imagined herself abroad:

'Her Britannic Majesty's
Secretary of State
Requests and requires
in the Name of Her Majesty
all those whom it may concern
to allow the bearer to pass freely
without let or hindrance,
and to afford the bearer

such assistance and protection
as may be necessary.'

"Sock it to 'em, Whittaker," she exhorted. Go give 'em hell.

The Consul returned looking reassuringly cheerful. "I've had a word with the *Marsciallo* and explained the circumstances," he said. "It would appear that your attire and behaviour - and that of your two companions, led an elderly man walking his dog in the woods to draw the wrong conclusions about your activities. He reported his suspicions to the *Carabinieri.*"

"What did he think we were doing?" asked Dotty, puzzled.

"Practising black magic," said the Consul.

"Good Lord!" exclaimed Dotty.

"This is still a very superstitious country," he explained, "particularly in rural areas. Fear of the 'evil eye', belief in astrologers and fortune-tellers is still prevalent. Generally, it's harmless *white* magic - young girls placing a few hairs from a boyfriend's head beneath the mattress in the hope that the young man will 'pop the question'. But it's not at all uncommon, even in this day and age, to read of the police breaking up a coven; arresting very unpleasant people participating in black rites. The rope coated in molasses dangling from the tree, could have been mistaken for one to be used for a ritual hanging!"

Dotty remained silent, his words forcing her to consider for the first time how easy it was for innocent actions to be dangerously misinterpreted. What else could the man have imagined when he came across three masked figures dressed in black, wearing pointed hats and prancing around by lantern light, chanting incantations. They were lucky he hadn't suffered a seizure.

"And," said the Consul, trying to maintain a disapproving expression, "there's the matter of the three mobility scooters that you and your friends *commandeered.*"

"Are they still missing?" asked Dotty, looking ashamed, concerned that a couple of guests would be confined to quarters.

"They were retrieved last night," he replied.

"I won't cause any more trouble," said Dotty. "I was going home today anyway."

"I know," said the Consul. "You seem to have made a lot of friends at the hotel who clearly know more about how these things work in Italy than I do. Before I arrived this morning the receptionist had already sent the hall porter over here with your passport and plane ticket to confirm your identity and the flight you're booked on this evening."

"Good old Luigi," said Dotty happily.

Indeed, thought Whittaker, wondering about the

legality of charging across town clutching a foreigner's passport. But this was Italy, and if the *marasciallo* didn't raise an eyebrow, why should he? "There are a couple of formalities to deal with at the desk, and then I'll take you back to the hotel to pack," he said.

Emerging from the *Casermo,* the Consul shepherded Dotty to a car parked in the piazza.

"Is this it?" she asked, looking with disgust at the little Fiat.

Whittaker nodded as he opened the passenger door for her.

"I thought you'd have a Rolls Royce with the Union Jack fluttering," said Dotty, getting into the car with a bad grace.

"Not these days, I'm afraid," he replied, sounding almost as regretful as she did. "We operate on a tight budget."

"It's disgraceful," she said indignantly as he slid into the driving seat and folded his long legs up like an ironing board. "A man in your position. The way things are going you'll be on a bike next."

"Our chap in the Hague already is," he responded dryly.

"If it's any consolation, Mr. Whittaker," said Dotty "*you* still look the part."

"You're too kind, Mrs. Lucas."

On the short drive back to the hotel the Consul, not

wishing to be drawn into expressing an opinion about the rights or wrongs of her arrest and subsequent confinement, deflected her questions. "I'm sure your friends at the hotel will be better informed than I am," he said.

"Free at last!" exclaimed Luigi, smiling broadly as Dotty and the Consul walked up to the desk.

"The Marshmallow said I could go," replied Dotty.

"The who?" asked Luigi.

"The man in charge - with all the braid," said Dotty.

Luigi laughed. "The *Marasciallo,* ma-ra-shi-allo, " he corrected her, pronouncing the name phonetically.

"I was close," said Dotty. "This is Mr. Whittaker," she continued proudly, "the British Consul."

The men acknowledged one another.

"Where are Sandro and Pietro?" Dotty asked.

"Later signora," said Luigi, inhibited by the presence of Whittaker who, sensing this, and keen to get back to the Consulate, took his leave. He handed Dotty her passport and plane ticket.

"I have asked my uncle, who has a taxi service, to take signora Lucas to the airport this evening," Luigi assured him. "She will be safe in our hands."

"Don't worry Mr. Whittaker," said Dotty. "I'll be on the plane. I wouldn't dream of doing anything to embarrass *you.*"

The Consul smiled. He'd taken a liking to this feisty woman who, in her own unconventional way, was determined to make the most of her widowhood, and who was treated with such obvious affection by the staff.

"Goodbye, Mrs. Lucas," he said, as they shook hands.

"Thank you very much for rescuing me," said Dotty. "The Queen must be proud of you."

"I think it's more thanks to your Italian friends here than it is to me," he replied.

"As we're in Italy," said Dotty, "would you mind if I said goodbye in the continental way?"

"And what way would that be?" asked Whittaker.

Dotty stood on her toes and kissed him on both cheeks. "I just wanted to add that to my holiday memories," she said, blushing. "Kissing a Consul!"

Although Luigi had the needs of the other guests to consider, he nevertheless couldn't wait to hear the details of Dotty's incarceration, and she in turn was eager for him to fill in the missing pieces. Summoning an assistant from accounts, and keeping an eye out for the manager, he whisked her off to the spa annexe which was deserted at that time of the day.

Ten minutes later he returned to his duties and Dotty, her head buzzing, looked at her watch. If she didn't get a move on soon she'd never fit everything in before her departure.

Sandro and Pietro, Luigi had reassured her, had been released by the time Whittaker arrived at the *Casermo* and would by now have joined the rest of the troupe in Bassano, where they were performing that evening. She'd feared that in the chaos of their arrest in the woods, their moth-splattered capes would have been trampled underfoot. Scanning the letter Sandro had left for her at Reception, she learned, to her relief, that he and Pietro had returned to the woods on their way back to the hotel and had retrieved the capes from the bushes where they'd had the presence of mind to hide them the previous night. Her cape, which had been torn off by the bemused *Carabinieri* and taken in evidence, had, no doubt, been consigned to the dustbin.

She went in search of Professor Albrecht. The conference had broken for lunch and he was sitting contentedly in his favourite spot under the trees beside the swimming pool. He beamed at the sight of her.

"Did we catch a Red Underwing?" asked Dotty, knowing that Sandro had handed the capes over to the Professor.

He nodded happily. "It was a bit.. how do you say... *moth-eaten* after its night in the woods," he replied, "but it is *wunderbar* to have two."

"Two?" queried Dotty.

"It was not Helga's fault," he replied, looking contrite. "I had put *my* specimen in a place so safe I could not find it. It was only this morning when the mini-bar was restocked that the maid found it behind the bottles of mineral water."

"I must apologise to Helga," said Dotty. "I was wrong to suspect her."

"She is not here," said the Professor. "I am sad to say she may still be hovering *zwischen himmel und erde* - between heaven and earth."

"Good Lord!" said Dotty. "I'd no idea she'd been taken ill. Will she live?"

The Professor looked startled; then shook his head, trying to hide his amusement. "No, no," he said, "I will explain. Sandro was concerned that if Helga was in the hotel she might learn of your planned adventure in the woods, so early yesterday evening Fiametta invited Helga to accompany her to a hot-air balloon rally near Padova. As you know, Helga is very interested in natural energy and was most eager to fly in a balloon. Unfortunately, conditions were not ideal and the wind was such that…" He paused.

"Go on," prompted Dotty, unable to bear the suspense.

"If my calculations regarding the thermal currents last night are accurate," said the Professor, struggling to retain his composure, "Helga could be somewhere over Austria by now."

After lunch with the Professor at the salad bar, Dotty returned to her room. Exhausted by the events of the previous twenty-four hours, she collapsed onto her bed for a much needed siesta. In the late afternoon she reluctantly tackled the melancholy chore of packing her suitcase. Roberto had gone. Sandro and his merry troupe had gone. The Ferrari was safely back in Modena. And now she was about to leave. There was a sense of completeness - and of emptiness.

She was relieved, now, that she had to return home. It would have been impossible for her to move straight on to Spain. She needed time to assimilate the experiences of the past ten days and the buried emotions they'd laid bare. She slipped the folder of photographs that Sandro had taken in Milan into her handbag, imagining their reactions when she proudly showed them to Angela and Jenny. The film in her camera was yet to be developed: photographs of the hotel, the Professor, Luigi, the Ferrari - and of Roberto, she thought with a stab of pain, as she slipped Ronald's photograph into her hand luggage.

She stepped onto the balcony and stared out over the gardens determined that *this* picture, in all its glorious technicolour, would be forever imprinted on her memory.

Reluctantly turning her back on the view, she strode

briskly across the room, leaving her suitcase and Salvatore hat box for the porter to collect, and opened her bedroom door.

She paused and looked up for the last time at the frolicking cherubs. If her son-in-law hadn't interfered, perhaps they would have looked down on her and Roberto: at life imitating art.

The taxi was waiting. Her luggage was in the boot. Dotty held out her hand to Luigi.

"Thank you for everything," she said, her eyes filling with tears. "I've had a wonderful time."

Luigi took her hand and squeezed it. "It has been a great pleasure to have you with us," he said. "We hope you will come again." He reached down behind the reception desk and brought up a large bouquet of long-stemmed red roses, which he passed to Dotty. "signore Carducci asked me to order them for you before he left yesterday morning."

Dotty opened the tiny envelope pinned to the cellophane and removed the card. *"Grazie per la memoria. Con affetto. Roberto."* -Thank you for the memory. With affection, Roberto, she read. There was no need to ask Luigi to translate. She knew enough Italian now to understand his words - and the sentiments they expressed.

The evening plane was only half-full and the soft

hum of its engines lulled Dotty into a reverie. I'm suspended between two worlds, she mused, peering down through the window as the aircraft cruised above the Alps, idly scanning the skies for a colourful bubble from which poor Helga might still be suspended.

When she'd apologised to Luigi for causing such disruption, he'd dismissed her concern with a grin. "This is a small community," he'd said. "You have given everyone lots to talk about. You have made them very happy."

I'd have preferred to do it in other ways, thought Dotty. What with one thing and another, she couldn't have made her presence felt more widely during her stay if she'd hired a light aircraft and towed a banner across the skies of Italy emblazoned with the warning: *HEADS DOWN. HERE COMES DEMENTED DOTTY.*

Being arrested on suspicion of practising black magic was certainly one for the memoirs. She'd never known a bush telegraph like it. An officer in the *Carabinieri* had told his cousin who was a gardener at the hotel who'd told Luigi, who'd told his sister, and by the morning everyone in Bellarosa knew. "The *Carabinieri* could not release the three of you until they had been seen to make a proper investigation and satisfied themselves that what everyone was telling them was true," Luigi had said, 'otherwise they would have suffered a loss of face."

And to be fair, thought Dotty, it wasn't *their* fault. They were only doing their duty.

Her reverie was shattered by a bony finger digging into her shoulder.

"Surprise, surprise!" said Nelly Broadbent.

"Oh no, not you again," said Dotty.

"Charming," replied Nelly, undeterred. "I was last on. Only spotted you when I went to the loo. Mind if I join you?"

"Feel free," said Dotty, secretly welcoming the distraction.

"Given up on your European tour?" asked Nelly, slipping into the seat beside her.

"Nope," said Dotty. "I have to return home for a while to sort out a property matter. What about you? "

Nelly shook her head. "I'm going straight," she said. "Turned over the proverbial."

Dotty snorted in disbelief. "Pull the other one," she said.

"Your cynicism does you no credit, Dorothy," said Nelly, who was looking irritatingly pleased with herself.

"I suppose the priest gave you a talking to at Confession - about Romolo," said Dotty. "Said it was time to mend your ways."

"Didn't get a chance to confess," replied Nelly, delighted at being given the opening to tell all.

"Everything moved too fast. Word soon got out in Bellarosa and spread like measles. Before you could say 'Holy Hot Dog' pilgrims were arriving and the place was turning into a shrine, so..." Nelly paused and stared dreamily into space.

"So...what?"

"I'm going to run a little shop in Bellarosa with one of Arturo's nephews, - selling religious souvenirs: painted wall plates of Romolo gazing up at St. Anthony; paperweights; china replicas of the dog with a ham bone in his mouth to put on the mantelpiece; T-shirts...All very tasteful. And we'll make regular donations to the convent from the profits. I'm just going back to the UK to make sure my son is still where he's supposed to be before starting my new career."

"You're going to keep up this pretence of being a nun?"

"Don't be daft," said Nelly, "No one will recognise me in mufti."

The stewardess appeared in the aisle and handed them an evening snack in small plastic boxes. Dotty slammed her hand down hard on the top of Nelly's unopened container.

"No 'just for old time's sake'," she warned her.

"I wouldn't dream of it," said Nelly. I'm going to be a Whoopie."

It was raining, the skies the colour of pewter, as the taxi pulled away from Belmont Avenue and a damp and depressed Dotty turned the key in the front door of the house she'd left without a backward glance. What a contrast, she thought, stepping over a pile of junk mail into a silent, musty hall. Where's the sunshine; the animation; the laughter? I've been away for less than a fortnight and yet it seems like a lifetime. Stop whinging, she told herself. You've hardly crossed the threshold. You've got a £30,000 windfall. She telephoned Angela and Jenny. "It's Mum," she said. "I'm back."

Dotty was slumped in a shabby chair staring into space. She'd gone through the motions: taken her luggage upstairs, put a hot-water bottle in her bed; found a carton of Long Life milk and made herself a cup of tea. A key turned in the lock and she looked up as Angela, Richard and Jenny came rushing in..

"Here sits the armchair traveller," she said, slowly getting to her feet as Angela opened her arms to embrace her.

"Why didn't you let us know when you were arriving?" Angela asked. "We'd have met you at the airport. You could have stayed the night with us."

"Thanks very much," said Dotty, "but coming back, I felt a bit like a diver surfacing with the bends. Better to decompress on my own."

"It's only a temporary blip, Gran," said Richard, enveloping her in a bear hug. "You'll soon be frightening the natives again. Anyway, it's great to see you."

"It's great to see you too," said Dotty, her spirits rising.

"Welcome home. And about time too," said Jenny, clinging on to her mother. "It's wonderful news about the house and don't take any notice of Richard. You can stay here now, where you belong."

Some things never change, thought Dotty, and why should they? However predictable her daughter's reaction might be, she was still glad to see her.

"I like the new hairstyle, Mum," Angela called from the kitchen where she was unpacking a carrier bag she'd brought in containing milk, bacon and eggs, butter and bread from her fridge.

"I'll tell you everything tomorrow," replied Dotty, joining her. "I'm a bit weary now."

Angela glanced over her shoulder to check that Jenny couldn't overhear. "You'll have no trouble selling the house again," she whispered. "And in the meantime you could prepare a bit more: perhaps take some foreign language lessons. There's even an opera appreciation class starting next Monday in the church hall. You might enjoy that now you've had a taste of Italy."

Dotty thought it would be quite a while before she

could appreciate something in which everybody died singing. Still, it *was* good to be home.

CHAPTER TWENTY

For a brief time my life's been like a rich, iced fruitcake with cherries on top, thought Dotty miserably as she set off the following morning to stock up on food, and now it's turned back into a stale Victoria sponge with not much jam in the middle.

She called in at Painless Travel to cancel the rest of her travel itinerary.

"I thought you'd see sense," said Nigel - which was a mistake.

`"I have only one word to say to you," replied Dotty. "Ferrari."

She continued on to the cemetery to say hello to Ronald. Unable to face tramping through the sodden garden to cut flowers, she bought a bunch from the florists on the corner. Ronald wouldn't have approved, but then a lot had happened recently that would have had him turning in his grave. She was pleased to see that her daughters had visited their father in her absence and that the celery and parsley arrangement had been replaced by rain-dashed lilies. That wasn't the only change: vivid green shoots were pushing their way up through the grave mound. The onions she'd lobbed in after the coffin had been lowered were sprouting. She smiled. Even in death, Ronald was still the champ.

Mindful of her conversation with Nick in Italy, she threw herself into ruthlessly clearing out years of accumulated junk in readiness for the resale of the house, and in the knowledge that wherever she moved to next she wouldn't have the space to accommodate it even if she wanted to. The dustman will have a hernia, she thought, as she surveyed the black rubbish bags. She added a couple more which she'd had second thoughts about donating to Oxfam; fearing that the earnest lady in charge of the shop would take one look at their mothball-reeking contents and ask her if she was in need of charity herself.

How wrong she'd be. She took Richard shopping one Saturday and spent some of her windfall treating him to a laptop computer; insisting that he choose exactly the model he wanted so long as he didn't try to explain to her how it worked. "Dad will say you're spoiling me," he said. "Good," she replied.

She entertained Margaret with a censored version of her Italian holiday experiences and fended off the vicar when he dropped broad hints that she should resume her voluntary duties at church. She had no wish to lapse into the old routine. She was determined that her return should be, as Richard had said, "a temporary blip."

Angela and Jenny were entranced by the photographs of her make-over and her descriptions of

Salvatore and Sandro. She couldn't bring herself to have the film in her own camera developed yet, or indeed to mention Roberto. On their part, neither of her daughters mentioned the Ferrari, leading Dotty to the conclusion that although they suspected they hadn't been told the whole truth about Paul and Nick's visit, they'd thought it wiser to let the matter rest.

Eating alone most evenings, her thoughts inevitably returned to Roberto. They hadn't anticipated that their final hours together would be so brutally cut short, but still, why *had* he departed without leaving his address? Because he had no wish to stay in touch, she told herself. It was just a holiday romance. "Thank you for the *memory*," he'd written in his note. She mustn't spoil *her* memory of their time together by wallowing in self-pity.

Feeling increasingly restless, she decided to accept a friend's invitation to visit her in Durham for a few days. Returning from the butcher's one afternoon, she stopped off at Painless Travel to collect a train timetable. Pausing outside the glass door, she saw a man, his back to her, standing by Nigel's desk, a suitcase on the floor beside him.

For a fraction of a heart-bursting second, she was convinced it was Roberto. I've got to stop this, she admonished herself, I'm seeing him everywhere. They're going to carry me off soon if I don't pull myself together.

But it was no hallucination.

"Good morning," he said formally, as he stood to one side to allow her to enter, having immediately picked up something in her expression which warned him against revealing they were acquainted.

"Good morning," replied Dotty, desperately trying to control her feelings.

"I have just arrived," said Roberto, "I am looking for accommodation. What you call bed and breakfast."

"I've told him it's impossible," said Nigel. Having mentally dismissed Roberto, he'd given Dotty only the briefest of glances before returning his attention to his computer screen. "Strictly residential, this neighbourhood. There's nowhere around here."

"Oh yes there is," Dotty blurted out before her legs gave way beneath her. "I do bed and breakfast. And dinner."

"No you do not, Mrs. Lucas," said Nigel, looking aghast.

She leaned across his desk. "I've got news for you, Nigel," she said. "I do now!"

"He's foreign." Nigel mouthed.

"I know," said Dotty, looked pleased. "And if you go telling tales to my family again, I'll throttle you with your own bow tie."

Without another word, fearing that this was all a

dream and she'd wake up at any second, she turned abruptly and headed for the door, Roberto following close behind.

"Well," she said, once they were outside, her joy so uncontainable she feared she might spontaneously combust, "I can hardly believe it. It really is you!"

Roberto smiled. "It really is me," he said.

"The flowers...the...." burbled Dotty, "I didn't expect that you..."

Roberto, conscious that the pair of them were blocking the pavement, picked up his suitcase. "Which way?" he asked.

Dotty pointed to her left and slipped her arm through his.

"I was coming in from the terrace when your son-in-law arrived. When I saw him going up the stairs to your room with you I thought it was better not to get involved. But later...I telephoned Luigi who said you had returned home instead of going to Spain. He gave me your address. It is against the rules but he did not think that you would mind."

"But why didn't you telephone?" persisted Dotty, thinking of her proposed trip to Durham. "I might have been away again."

Roberto shrugged. "Mebbi I say I will come. Mebbi next day I am struck by lightning...who knows...I thought I would find a little place to stay close by, then I could call on you without obligation. And," he added, "a surprise is better."

"I remember," said Dotty, "Second rule of life. Never, never make plans."

"That's right," replied Roberto.

"Just my luck," groaned Dotty, as Margaret emerged from the butchers, her eyes swivelling frantically between Dotty's arm clinging on to Roberto's and the suitcase he was carrying.

Dotty had no choice but to introduce them,

Margaret blushed, feasting her eyes on Roberto as he took her hand and bowed elegantly over it.

"Don't move, Margaret," warned Dotty, "or you'll tread on your eyes."

"I love Italy," said Margaret, ignoring Dotty, her attention elsewhere. "Such a beautiful country."

"Thank you," said Roberto, "You know my country well?"

"Oh yes," simpered Margaret.

"I would have thought five days in Rimini with the Fellowship Group was no more than a passing acquaintance myself," said Dotty, with a waspishness that caused Roberto to raise his eyebrows.

****

Roberto glanced at his watch on the bedside table in the guest room. 6.30 am. It was unlikely Dotty would be awake at this time. He could enjoy his usual morning ritual of drinking his first *espresso* of the day alone. To ensure his daily fix, he'd packed a two-cup Mocha coffee maker and half a kilo of coffee in his suitcase. Tea was only for invalids, and he didn't trust the English when it came to coffee. He silently crept downstairs.

Dotty glanced at the bedside clock on the table beside the marital bed. It was early. Tip-toeing to her bedroom door she opened it silently and listened. Roberto must still be asleep. If she washed and dressed quickly the bathroom would be free when he awoke. If he was anything like Ronald in the morning, he'd establish squatter's rights. For the first few weeks after Ronald's death, she'd found herself pausing outside the bathroom door, her half-asleep brain still programmed to yell " Have you taken root in there, Ronald?" before sad realisation woke her up.

Bathed and dressed, she sat at her dressing table and stared at her reflection in the mirror. Do I look different? she wondered. Do my eyes give me away? Will anybody guess? The last time she'd asked herself that question, she'd been 16, trying to sneak in without her parents seeing her after her first goodnight kiss on the doorstep.

The previous evening she'd laid the kitchen table with a spotless damask cloth that had belonged to her mother. Somewhat self-consciously, she'd lit candles in a pair of tarnished silver-plated candlesticks she'd unearthed during her clear-out. On the way home that morning they'd called at the off licence and Roberto had bought a couple of bottles of Italian wine. Unsure of Dotty's culinary talents, he'd offered to cook dinner.

Dotty had sat at the kitchen table, watching him bustling around wearing one of her aprons, creating, on the surface, an atmosphere of cosy domesticity. But there was an emotional undercurrent of romantic celebration, and an unspoken, but nevertheless potent acknowledgement that they were about to pick up their relationship where it had been so abruptly broken off.

As the clock on the tower of St. Botolph's struck midnight, she'd paused with Roberto outside the door to the guest room, intending to say 'good night'. But she hadn't been given a chance to say 'goodnight'.

Afterwards, her somewhat speedy return to the empty marital bed had somehow seemed the right thing to do: not only as a courtesy she instinctively wished to extend to Ronald but also because of a sudden insight which she still found confusing: the revelation that *sleeping* beside another man in the home she had shared with Ronald would have been a more intimate act than the sex that had preceded it.

Since her return from Bellarosa she'd fantasised more times than she cared to admit about what might have taken place if her son-in-law hadn't behaved like a drunken cuckoo in the nest. There had been a bit of self-conscious thrashing around at the outset: a tangle of what seemed more than the normal compliment of arms and legs getting in the way; the clumsiness of bodies grown accustomed, however unwillingly, to abstinence; but they'd managed very nicely after that. It had been comforting to feel a warm body against hers once more.

And that, thought Dotty, as she re-made her bed, had been another revelation. It had been *comforting*. Who would have imagined it. You live and learn. All those girlish assumptions about passionate Latin lovers and undemonstrative Englishmen had been well and truly shattered. In or out of bed Ronald was definitely still The Champ!

Roberto, looking like a matinee idol in his navy silk dressing gown fetchingly piped in scarlet, was strolling through the garden, enjoying the early morning sun. What a tragedy, he thought, contemplating the wilderness around him: the rampant weeds choking the flower beds, the rows of bolting lettuces and rotting marrows; so much good food going to waste.

Crossing over to the garden shed, he noticed that the door was ajar. He stepped inside and stood in silent, approving contemplation of Ronald's gardening tools hanging from regimented rows of hooks perfectly aligned along the walls of the shed before shaking his head in sorrow at the rusting bloom on many of the tools. A man who took such pride in his garden would never have allowed that to happen. Roberto sighed. How could Dotty show such careless lack of concern in allowing the proverbially damp English weather to invade Ronald's sanctuary, he wondered; unaware that the last time she'd entered the shed had been immediately after Ronald's death when she'd had more on her mind than securing the latch.

P.C. Geoffrey Whitlow, leaving the house next door to go on duty, heard a noise in Mrs. Lucas's garden. He glanced at his watch. Having done it from childhood, he silently shinned up the dividing fence and climbed into the Lucas's big old pear tree. Peering down with some difficulty through the foliage he saw the top of a man's head emerging from the garden shed and a brief glimpse of the lawn mower he was pushing ahead of him in the direction of the back gate. As the man trundled the machine along the path below him, Geoffrey dropped from the branch onto an unsuspecting Roberto, emitting a blood-curdling yell of "Gotcha!"

"*Aiuto! Aiuto*" - Help! yelled a terrified Roberto, who had fallen awkwardly. Struggling back to his feet, he was no match for this youthful assailant, who grabbed a handful of his dressing gown with one hand, yanked the tasselled cord from around him with the other, and pushed him forcefully back against the tree. At the sight of a police uniform, Roberto limply offered no further resistance as Geoffrey encircled him with the cord and lashed him to the trunk of the pear tree.

Attracted by the noise, Dotty came rushing down the garden. She stopped in her tracks at the scene which confronted her.

"Don't you think you're a bit old to be playing Cowboys and Indians, Geoffrey?" she asked.

"Catching villains is not a game, Mrs. Lucas," he replied. "I have just apprehended an intruder on your property. He was stealing your lawnmower."

"*You're* the intruder, you clot!" said Dotty. "Since when have thieves swanned around the suburbs wearing expensive silk dressing gowns? Who did you think he was? Cary Grant?"

"Who's Cary Grant?" asked Geoffrey.

Roberto, still tied to the tree, was far from pleased at being ignored. "Please forgive me for intruding on your interesting conversation," he interrupted, his voice dripping with sarcasm, "but if you could spare a moment to..."

"Oh sorry, Roberto," said Dotty, rushing forward to untie him.

Snatching the cord from her hand he tied it tightly around his waist. Encouraged by Dotty's far from respectful response to the forces of law and order, he turned his fury on Geoffrey. "What kind of country is this," he demanded, "where a man cannot walk in the garden without policemen dropping out of the trees like Tarzans?"

"Are you *still* climbing our pear tree, Geoffrey?" asked Dotty.

"I was effecting entry by the fastest possible route," he replied.

"*Somebody*," said Roberto, looking accusingly at Dotty, "had left the door of the garden shed open. I was wanting to give the lawnmower some sunshine and dry air. *Guarda!* - look at my robe," he moaned, near to tears, lifting a muscular arm exposed by a ripped sleeve. With a curt nod, protectively holding the tattered remnants of his Valentino around him, he limped off with as much dignity as he could muster in the direction of the house.

"You want to watch it from now on, Geoffrey," said Dotty. "He's Italian and you know what Italians are like. Upset him again and you're going to find yourself one moonless night tied to a lump of concrete at the bottom of your goldfish pond."

"I'm sorry, Mrs. Lucas," said Geoffrey. "I only saw the top of his head before I fell on him. I couldn't see what he was wearing. I was only trying to protect you."

Dotty, seeing his earnest expression, felt ashamed

of her outburst. "No, *Constable,*" she said, "*I'm* the one who should apologise to *you.* I shouldn't have been so flippant. I'm grateful for your concern. You're a very good policeman."

"Thank you," said Geoffrey.

"Now buzz off," said Dotty, "and issue a few parking tickets!"

Turning abruptly on her heels, she headed for the kitchen door.

Will I ever be allowed to lead my life without everybody interfering, thought Dotty, tears springing into her eyes as she entered the kitchen. There was no sign of Roberto. In all likelihood he was packing his suitcase, unwilling to risk life and limb any longer in this madhouse. She walked into the hall and stood at the bottom of the stairs, listening. He was running a bath. Thanks to Geoffrey, a blossoming romance looked like turning into a one-night stand.

Dotty was making toast when Roberto walked into the kitchen. He was immaculately clad in English country clothes: corduroy trousers, checked shirt and highly polished brogues, but the cut of the clothes was distinctly Italian.

"I'm sorry about what happened," she said, "Were you hurt?"

He shook his head. "Sometimes, I dunno. I'd forgotten how dangerous it was to be with you," he replied.

"You said last night you'd missed me because I made you feel young again," said Dotty.

Roberto smiled. "That was last night. Today I think mebbi you are all trying to finish me off."

"You must let me buy you a new dressing gown," said Dotty.

"Forget about it," said Roberto. "It wasn't your fault. But mebbi you could tell your bodyguard to stay away from me from now on."

There was a timid knock on the kitchen door. Dotty opened it to find Nigel standing on the doorstep, clutching a leaflet.

"Morning Mrs. Lucas," he said "It's me, Nigel. I thought you'd like a copy of the updated local bus timetable."

"How very, very thoughtful of you Nigel. Do come in," said Dotty, stepping to one side to allow him to enter the kitchen. "You mustn't leave without meeting the *real* reason for your dawn delivery."

"I just wanted to make sure...I mean..." Intimidated by Roberto's steely gaze, Nigel was about to turn tail when his escape route was blocked by the arrival of Angela and Richard.

"Good morning Mum," said Angela, gaily. "I'm on my way to drop Richard at school so I thought we'd pop in for a minute."

"Morning Angela, Richard," said Dotty, not

remotely surprised at their sudden appearance.

"Hello Gran," said Richard, giving his grandmother a hug as Jenny and Nick appeared.

"Hello Mum," said Jenny, squeezing into the kitchen.

"Morning Jenny. Morning Nick," said Dotty, as Paul poked his head around the door.

"Good morning," said Paul.

"Goodbye," said Dotty.

"Paul," said Angela, "you told me you were going straight to the office."

Everyone stared at Roberto, who had risen from the table.

"What a fortunate woman I am to be surrounded by such love," said Dotty. "How many other mothers would expect a visit from their entire family before break of day." She turned to Roberto. "Meet rent-a-mob."

"Ah," said Roberto, turning on the charm, "*che piacere*! What a pleasure."

"As you are no doubt aware," said Dotty, turning to her assembled family, "this is my friend, Roberto Carducci." She introduced Angela and Jenny.

Roberto took Angela's hand and kissed it before doing the same with Jenny's.

"My compliments Dorothea," said Roberto. "You have two beautiful daughters. They are taking after their mother."

"And this," said Dotty deliberately introducing a reluctant Paul after Nick and Richard had shaken hands with Roberto, "is my son-in-law, Paul. I'm sure you remember Paul."

"Of course," said Roberto, his mouth smiling but his eyes refusing to join in. "I saw you the evening of your arrival at the Hotel Palladio."

The colour drained from Paul's face. "I must go," he said, glancing at his watch, "It's later than I..."

Dotty grabbed his arm. "Five more minutes won't matter will it," she said softly, but her determined expression brooked no argument.

"Now," said Roberto, with studied politeness, trying to make his way through the throng to the kitchen door, "I must not intrude further on this family reunion. If you will excuse me I have much work to do in the garden. I hope we will meet again very soon."

Dotty turned to Nigel. "Sneak!" she hissed, as soon as Roberto was out of earshot. "I warned you."

"It wasn't me," he whimpered.

"Right," she said, looking grim. "Hands up whoever has spoken to Margaret."

Jenny reluctantly raised her hand. "I bumped into her half an hour ago in the newsagent's. I'd run out of milk for breakfast."

"So you picked up the telephone to your sister. What a boring life you must lead," said Dotty as

Jenny looked at her feet. "Very well. Now you're all here, we're going to sort this out once and for all. SIT DOWN!"

There was a mad scramble for chairs. Nigel shrank back against the wall trying to make himself invisible in the space between the back door and the side of the old kitchen dresser. Dotty stood in front of the sink, facing them; arms folded like a battle-axe.

"You must understand our concern..." Paul began.

"*SILENZIO*!!!" shouted Dotty. "That's Italian for 'silence', and I intend to learn many more Italian words because Roberto is going to stay for as long as he and I wish."

"Great!" said Richard, taking her side, "We're studying Julius Caesar this term. He could help me with..."

"I don't think passing your examination should be dependent upon your grandmother playing fast and loose," Paul cut in with risible primness, glaring at Angela and Nick who couldn't hide their amusement.

"I see," said Dotty, "no sex for the over sixties, is that it?"

"You're going to be late for school, Richard," said Paul, "And," he enquired, suddenly registering Nigel's presence, "why are you still here?"

Nigel's cheeks flamed with embarrassment. "I'm ever so sorry," he said, "I shouldn't have intruded. I'll go now. It's just that I've never met a family like this

- 273 -

before. It's riveting."

"Bit different from yours, is it Nigel?" asked Angela.

"There's only me and my mum," said Nigel solemnly. "She doesn't say much. She's got varicose veins."

"Stay where you are, Nigel," said Angela sweetly, "we've been through a lot together. You're one of the family now."

"Really?" said Nigel, thrilled. "Does that include my mum as well?"

Angela nodded. Nigel beamed.

"When you've finished bonding," said Dotty, "perhaps I could be allowed to continue. Unless you want me to leave my money to a donkey sanctuary I suggest you finally get it into your silly heads that my life is my own. I shall invite whoever I wish to stay beneath *my* roof. Roberto has offered to clear up the mess in the garden and he loves cooking. If this is what european unity's all about, it's certainly got *my* vote."

"I don't think this is quite what the Commissioners in Brussels had in mind," said Paul.

"Oh do shut up, Paul," said Angela.

"We spent a lot of time together in Italy," continued Dotty. "I hired the Ferrari for Roberto. I'm sure Paul hasn't forgotten *that*," she added, unable to resist another dig at her son-in-law.

"The gigolo," murmured Jenny, looking pointedly at Paul.

"Some gigolo," said Angela. "Wow!"

"Is it like this all the time?" piped up Nigel, emboldened by his acceptance into the family. "I'm emotionally drained."

Jenny indicated to Nick that she'd get a lift to her office with Angela and Richard. Once they'd driven away and Nigel had wobbled off on his bike, Paul poked his head through the window of Nick's Porsche.

"She shouldn't be alone in the house with that man," said Paul. "What will the neighbours think? I wish I could make her see sense."

"It'd be easier to stop a runaway truck," said Nick, "although it beats me what women see in these ageing Latin lovers. Silver hair and skin like a crocodile handbag - and they're falling all over themselves. Jenny and Angela were smitten."

"You're not serious," said Paul.

"You'd better believe it," said Nick. Jenny had never looked at *him* like that.

"And it won't stop here," said Paul sensing he was regaining Nick as an ally. "We've all heard about these extended Italian families. It's a big house. Next thing you know, there'll be cousins and uncles and heaven knows who arriving on the doorstep. Why follow her here, unless he's planning to take advantage of her?"

"And pocket the family inheritance?" asked Nick.

"That had never entered my head," said Paul, refusing to look him in the eye.

It wouldn't need to, thought Nick, recalling his discussion with Dotty at the Hotel Palladio. Whatever ructions the ageing Romeo might cause, there were other surprises on the way. It was all up to him now.

"I hope having me in your house is not going to be a big problem," said Roberto, emerging from the garden shed with a rake in his hand as Dotty walked down the garden path.

"They'll get used to it," she replied, relieved to see that he'd thought better of his fashion plate country look and replaced his brogues with a pair of Ronald's wellies. She couldn't face any further depletion of his wardrobe. "You're sure you haven't changed your mind about staying?"

"If you are happy, I am happy," he said. "It is not what I expected an English family to be like. I feel at home here."

"They shouldn't keep poking their noses into my business," said Dotty.

"You can't stop them," said Roberto. "That is what a family is *for.*"

After dropping Richard at the school gate, Angela drove Jenny to her office.

"I'd never have imagined Mum would go this far," said Jenny.

"I thought he was charming," said Angela.

"Sensational" agreed Jenny. "Those hazel eyes..."

"You're not planning to steal mother's lover are you?" Angela teased.

"You don't think they've..."

Angela shrugged. "Who knows! They must have spent a lot of time together in Italy, and he was obviously keen to see her again."

"She's too old for him," said Jenny.

"You mean he's wasted on an older woman," said Angela, glancing at her sister in amusement. "I like him for that; preferring a woman his own age to some young bimbo."

"It's weird to think of her being seduced," said Jenny. "It was difficult enough imagining Mum and Dad having sex when they were *our* age. Do you remember the day I came home from school after my class had been given The Facts of Life talk? I must have been about 10. I lay awake that night listening for noises from their bedroom, wondering if they might be doing 'it' when I heard Mum yell 'That's enough for now Ronald!' and Dad gasp, and I froze. Then Mum screamed 'I don't want to hear another word about your bug resistant cucumbers. Switch off the light.'" And then there was an almighty crash and the sound of glass breaking. She'd chucked his seed catalogue across the room and it had gone through the window!"

"I'd never realised when Dad was alive how frustrated Mum must have been with her life," said Angela, when they'd stopped laughing. "But you know, since he died she's played an absolute blinder. She's made thirty thousand pounds, had a crazy time in Italy and returned home with a handsome admirer."

"And forgotten Dad," said Jenny, suddenly remembering where her loyalty lay.

"Of course she hasn't," said Angela. "Don't start all that again. Dad's gone. Don't you want her to be happy?"

CHAPTER TWENTY-ONE

"He was a good man, your husband," said Roberto one morning, coming in from the garden. "A man who loved the earth. I think if I had known him we would have been friends." He placed a trug of vegetables and herbs on the kitchen table.

"What do you call those in Italian?" asked Dotty, pointing at the potatoes.

"*Patate.*"

"And broccoli?"

"*Broccoli.* And this is *spinacio* and that is *oregano.*"

"Huh!" said Dotty scornfully, "those are just English words you've mucked about with. *Patate, broccoli, spinacio,*" she repeated in a mocking sing-song voice. "Bit lazy not bothering to have words of your own."

"*Per favore!*" - please, protested Roberto. "It was you English who steal from the Italians - the Latino. My broccoli and spinach were there first. Before the Romans came to your country you was uncivilised barbarians."

"That's not true!" said Dotty

"It is true, I tell you!" he said. "In Italy we had culture and art and buildings covered with marble you can still see today. And what did you have? People going around in rags with their faces painted blue living in huts of straw."

"I think..." said Dotty.

"Don't think," said Roberto, "Men should do the thinking."

"What's Italian for 'arrogant?'" asked Dotty.

"*Arrogante!*" replied Roberto.

"English," said Dotty

"Italian," said Roberto.

"So you were arrogant first!" said Dotty, childishly.

"*Grazie!* - thank you," said Roberto playfully, amused by her vehemence.

But Dotty was not amused. She picked up her mug of tea and stalked out into the garden. She knew that the Italian and English names were virtually identical; she'd seen them on the menu at the Hotel Palladio. She couldn't care less which language laid claim to their *roots*. What had led her so childishly to provoke Roberto was that they were names of *vegetables*. The resentment had been building up inside her for the past few weeks and could no longer be contained.

Since his unexpected and welcome arrival at Belmont Avenue, Roberto had spent most of his time not with her but in the garden, rescuing it from months of neglect. The lawn had been mown to bowling green standard, weeds banished, perennials and vegetables given room to flourish, the garden tools oiled and polished. The compost heap looked like the leaning tower of Pisa. By the end of the third week, he'd made enough tomato puree to sink Naples.

He'd returned to the house each evening tired and content, with grubby hands and a look of smug satisfaction. After spending the next hour soaking his weary limbs in the bath, warbling his way through what must have been the entire repertoire of Puccini arias, he'd join her for dinner wearing yet another of the clean shirts which she'd dutifully washed and, bearing in mind his instruction to pay particular attention to the collars, ironed.

She'd initially been grateful for his offer to tidy up the garden, but before she'd realised what was happening, she'd automatically lapsed into her old, familiar routine: the grass widow busying herself with household chores while a Ronald clone concentrated his attention on the garden rather than her. Annoyed at herself for her instinctive acquiescence, she ruefully recalled something she'd read during the early days of feminism: 'You begin by sinking into his arms and end up with your arms in the sink."

She wanted to be seen in public with her handsome Italian lover, but Roberto had shrugged his shoulders when she'd suggested that they dine out one evening. There was no point in going to an Italian restaurant, he'd said, it would bear little resemblance to Italian cooking as he knew it. French? The French cuisine had evolved from the Italian cuisine. Did she know that? It was very interesting. English? What English cuisine? he had teased her. Why go out when there was so much good food in the garden going to waste?

But relief came unexpectedly. Roberto announced that he must return to Rome to await the birth of a new grandchild. Although family obligations took precedence, he tried, on the morning of his departure, to tentatively raise a matter which he'd been stewing along with his tomato puree.

Roberto knew that Dotty planned to re-sell the house. Where would she live once it was sold, he asked her in what he hoped was a tone of idle curiosity. Dotty shrugged.

"I cannot remember if I told you this," he said, "but I own an old stone farmhouse in Umbria - *Casa Concordia* - which has been in the family for generations. It is very sad, but none of my children want to live there. Isolated stone properties are of no interest to the younger generation. They think they are moving up in the world by moving down to modern houses in the valleys. Working in your garden, I have been thinking of what I have missed. I am tired of all the noise and confusion in Rome. But it would be lonely living in the country on my own..." He paused, his eyes on Dotty. "Of course, if I had someone with me, the house could be a home once more. There are fig, olive and walnut trees on the land. I could make a vegetable garden..."

And I could bottle your flaming produce, thought Dotty, remaining silent as she recalled his exclamation of delight when he'd walked into her pantry and seen the shelves laden with home-made jams, pickles, and bottled fruits. Although she'd accepted his compliments, she'd been aware of his surprise; of suddenly seeing her in a different light. The merry widow with a penchant for Ferraris and Milanese couture was, at heart, the next best thing to an Italian *mamma*.

Roberto broke the silence. "When you visit me in Rome," he said, "I will take you up to see the house. I think you will like it."

"I'm sure I will," murmured Dotty in non-committal tones.

It was ironic, she mused, that while she'd become increasingly resentful of Roberto for assuming that being a happy housewife should be the be-all and end-all of her life, the family had warmed to him for the same reason. Jenny had called in frequently and been treated by a shrewd Roberto with fatherly indulgence. Richard had enjoyed a number of animated conversations with him about Ancient Rome. Even Paul's concerns seemed to have been tempered by his admiration for the Italian's hard work in the garden and the dawning realisation that he was proving to be a stabilising influence on his wilful mother-in-law. Although nothing had been said,

Dotty sensed that Angela was the only one who suspected that her mother was becoming less enamoured.

In the weeks after Roberto returned to Rome, a seemingly endless procession of prospective purchasers tramped through the house; all equally obsessed by the quality of the plumbing. Was there a shower? Was the central heating efficient? The answer to both questions was "No", but Nick skilfully deflected such enquiries, drawing their attention to the house's original features: the tiled fireplaces, cast iron bath, the faded splendour of its Victorian conservatory.

He telephoned her one morning. "We're ready," he said.

"Oh Lord," said Dotty. "It's either decision time or pitching a tent on the common."

On the day contracts were exchanged on the sale of the house, Nick collected her in his Porsche and drove her to Safehaven, the retirement village. It had proved so popular that the complex had been extended and a dozen newly-built bungalows were now for sale.

Dotty only half-listened as Nick, wearing his funeral suit and black tie, and clutching a sheaf of sales particulars, extolled the virtues of Safehaven:

the beautifully manicured lawns; the health club, swimming pool, miniature golf-course and bowling green.

Returning to the car, Dotty paused in front of the sales board:

SAFEHAVEN RETIREMENT VILLAGE
FOR A DISCERNING AGE GROUP

Glancing around to ensure she wasn't being watched, she rooted around in her handbag and brought out a lipstick. Uncapping it, she added a couple of missing letters to the signboard. It now read:

SAFEHAVEN RETIREMENT VILLAGE
FOR A DISCERNING **CAGED** GROUP

Nick grinned. "You win," he said.

"There's nothing wrong with Safehaven," said Dotty. "I'm sure people are very happy here. But it's not for me."

"Come on," said Nick. "I've one more place to show you."

The following month, Dotty invited the family to Sunday lunch. Nick deliberately arrived late with Jenny to ensure that everyone else was present before they walked in.

"Nick's asked me to marry him and I've said yes!" Jenny announced, unable to contain her news as she rushed into the sitting room.

Dotty hugged her daughter. "This calls for champagne," she said, as Angela and Paul offered their congratulations. "Follow me, Richard."

"This is chilled," said Jenny suspiciously, when they returned with a tray and Richard handed her a brimming glass. "Nick said we were to keep it a secret until today."

"Wait," said Dotty, as glasses were raised and the happy couple toasted. "I have more good news. The house has been sold again. However..." She paused, seeing Jenny's face fall, "even though we've got the same price for the house, thanks to my future son-in-law's brilliant idea the sale also included only part of the land."

"But..." protested Jenny, "what..."

"Say one more word and you'll regret it," Dotty warned her. "Knowing how you couldn't bear the thought of my leaving, I agreed with Nick that this would be the next best thing. We've got planning permission to build a house where your father had his vegetable garden - for you and Nick."

"What a wonderful idea," said Angela.

"Excellent!" said Paul.

Jenny couldn't speak. Tears rolling down her

cheeks, she flung her arms around Nick. Dotty hoped she was weeping with joy and not snivelling in misery at the thought of digging up Ronald's turnips or she'd disown her.

When calm had been restored Dotty took the floor once more. "As you know," she said, "whatever money is left from the sale of this house will be shared equally between you two girls when I die. Obviously the building plot has been valued separately and Nick has bought Angela's half share." Reaching into her pocket she pulled out a cheque which she passed to her elder daughter. "That's yours," she said, "which should more than pay for Richard's university education."

"Thank you," said Paul, "I don't know what to say."

"That makes a change," said Dotty, smiling at him. She raised her glass. "Here's to Richard," she said, "and to a wild time at university."

"I don't think..." began Paul, before shrinking back in mock horror at the cries of "Shame!"

"Oh," said Dotty, "I nearly forgot." But she hadn't. "There's something else I must tell you..."

It was November when Dotty left Belmont Avenue with only the minimum of household essentials, her personal possessions, family mementoes and a few pieces of furniture. Angela and Jenny had taken what they wanted, and what remained had been sent to auction or dropped off at the Oxfam shop. With a sigh of relief, Dotty had donated most of the pantry store of jams and pickles and Roberto's gallons of tomato puree to St. Botolph's for the next Bring-and-Buy sale.

"I don't believe it!" Richard had exclaimed as she'd proudly shown the family her studio in a warehouse conversion overlooking the river in the centre of town. "Gran's got a pad!"

Now, waiting for the kettle to boil, she gazed in delight around her new home on Trafalgar Wharf, unable to believe her good fortune. Wooden floors, recessed lighting, a raised sleeping area separated by a sliding panel, a bathroom which would have given the one at the Hotel Palladio a run for its money. In place of faded chintz, dusty corners and countless panes of mottled conservatory glass to clean, she had a light-filled, virtually chore-free space and a generous balcony offering a bird's eye view of everything she was likely to need within walking distance. Who would have thought that one day she'd be standing in what the sales particulars described as a 'State-of-the-Art kitchen zone.'

"Beam me up, Scotty!" she murmured happily, patting the controls on the microwave oven. If she'd understood Richard correctly, it would scramble the eggs for her if she asked it nicely.

She took her mug of tea out onto the balcony.

Wrapping herself up in the ancient travelling rug, she contentedly settled herself in one of a pair of tatty old deckchairs which she'd also saved for sentimental reasons when she'd given the contents of Ronald's shed to members of the gardening club.

Sipping her tea, her thoughts reverted to Roberto. She hadn't yet come to terms with the knowledge that a man seemingly so different from Ronald could still feel the pull of his rural roots and that for a brief time during his visit her life had threatened to come full circle. She missed Roberto but, she accepted now, what she really missed was the relationship she'd enjoyed with him at the Hotel Palladio: a holiday romance divorced from the mundane demands of everyday life.

She'd read somewhere that widowers couldn't wait to re-marry; that they felt lost without their comfort blanket of domesticity. Many widows, however, were reluctant to commit themselves again once they'd tasted freedom; discovering, often to their surprise, that bereavement had granted them a new lease on life; that they no longer wished to be answerable to anyone else. Like a genie released from the bottle, her spirit could no longer be contained. She would visit Roberto. She wanted to see him again. She'd become very fond of him; but she hoped that by maintaining a distance between them rather than living side by side, they could recapture the pleasure of the days they'd spent together in Italy, in periodic romantic reunions.

Dotty picked out familiar landmarks as the setting sun gilded the gothic crenellations on the tower of the council offices and the glass-clad walls of the town's self-conscious claim to modernism - a junior skyscraper. If the day ever came when age or infirmity forced her to return to earth from her lofty perch and move into a retirement home, she'd take with her a store of memories, preserved like the bottled jams and pickles in her old pantry, which she could open one by one, savouring their concentrated flavour. I'm a very lucky woman, she thought. I've had the love and support of a kind and honest man for forty years. If that wasn't enough to be grateful for, I now I have a new home, a new life - and a new world beckons.

Resuming her original Grand Tour of Europe would have to wait until the spring; but there was just time for a special pre-Christmas treat: a week on a small island which had always been on her wish list.

Muffled up to the ears in a fake fur coat and matching hat, snowflakes swirling around her, Dotty stood on Brooklyn Bridge gazing across the water in awestruck contemplation of the stupendous cloud-piercing skyline of Manhattan.

"New York, New York!" she suddenly shouted in

exultation. "I'm ready for you!"

"But," asked Richard, standing equally awestruck beside her, "is New York ready for *you*?"

———————————

Printed in the United Kingdom by
Lightning Source UK Ltd., Milton Keynes
139071UK00001B/110/P